MARVEL

MARVEL ACTION
AVENGERS
THE FEAR EATERS

Marvel Publishing:

Jeff Youngquist: VP Production & Special Projects
Caitlin O'Connell: Assistant Editor, Special Projects
Sven Larsen: Director, Licensed Publishing
David Gabriel: SVP Print, Sales & Marketing
C.B. Cebulski: Editor In Chief
Joe Quesada: Chief Creative Officer
Dan Buckley: President, Marvel Entertainment
Alan Fine: Executive Producer

IDW Publishing:

Collection Edits
JUSTIN EISINGER
and **ALONZO SIMON**

Collection Design
CHRISTA MIESNER

Cover Art by
JON SOMMARIVA

Cover Colors by
PAC23

Chris Ryall, President and Publisher/CCO
Cara Morrison, Chief Financial Officer
Matt Ruzicka, Chief Accounting Officer
David Hedgecock, Associate Publisher
John Barber, Editor-In-Chief
Justin Eisinger, Editorial Director, Graphic Novels & Collections
Jerry Bennington, VP of New Product Development
Lorelei Bunjes, VP of Digital Services
Jud Meyers, Sales Director
Anna Morrow, Marketing Director
Tara McCrillis, Director of Design & Production
Mike Ford, Director of Operations
Rebekah Cahalin, General Manager

Ted Adams and Robbie Robbins, Founders of IDW

ISBN: 978-1-68405-581-4   23 22 21 20   1 2 3 4.

Special thanks: **Tom Brevoort**

Originally published as MARVEL ACTION: AVENGERS issues #7–9.

For international rights, contact licensing@idwpublishing.com

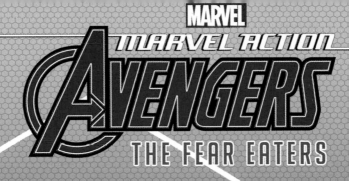

MARVEL

MARVEL ACTION AVENGERS

THE FEAR EATERS

WRITTEN BY MATTHEW K. MANNING

ART BY MARCIO FIORITO

COLORS BY PROTOBUNKER

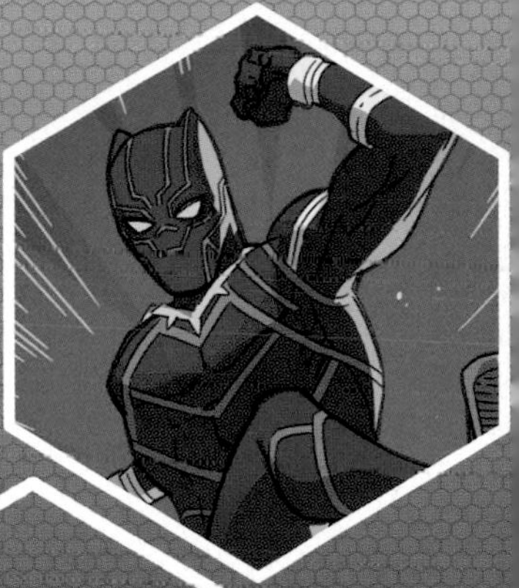

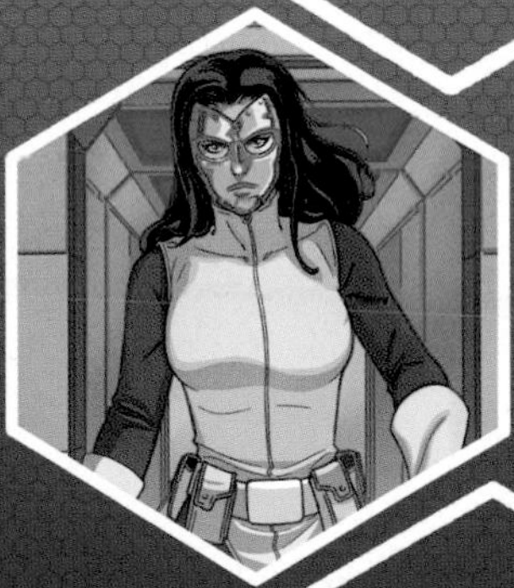

LETTERS BY CHRISTA MIESNER

ASSISTANT EDITS BY MEGAN BROWN

EDITED BY BOBBY CURNOW

EDITOR-IN-CHIEF JOHN BARBER

AVENGERS CREATED BY
STAN LEE & JACK KIRBY

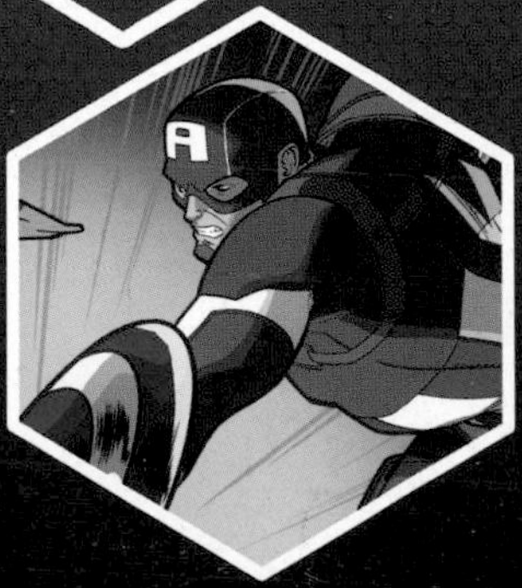

ART BY: JON SOMMARIVA
COLORS BY: PAC 23

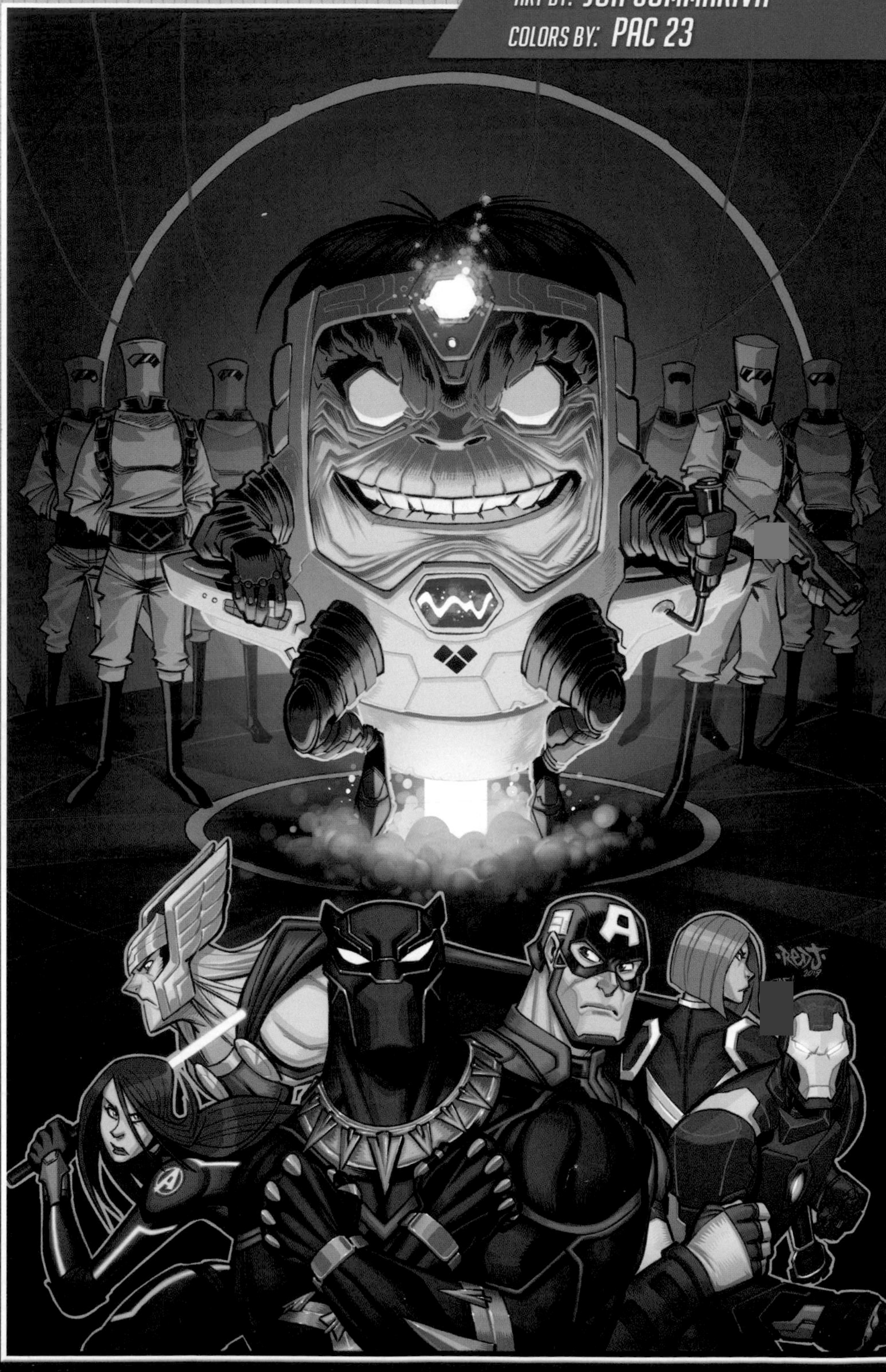

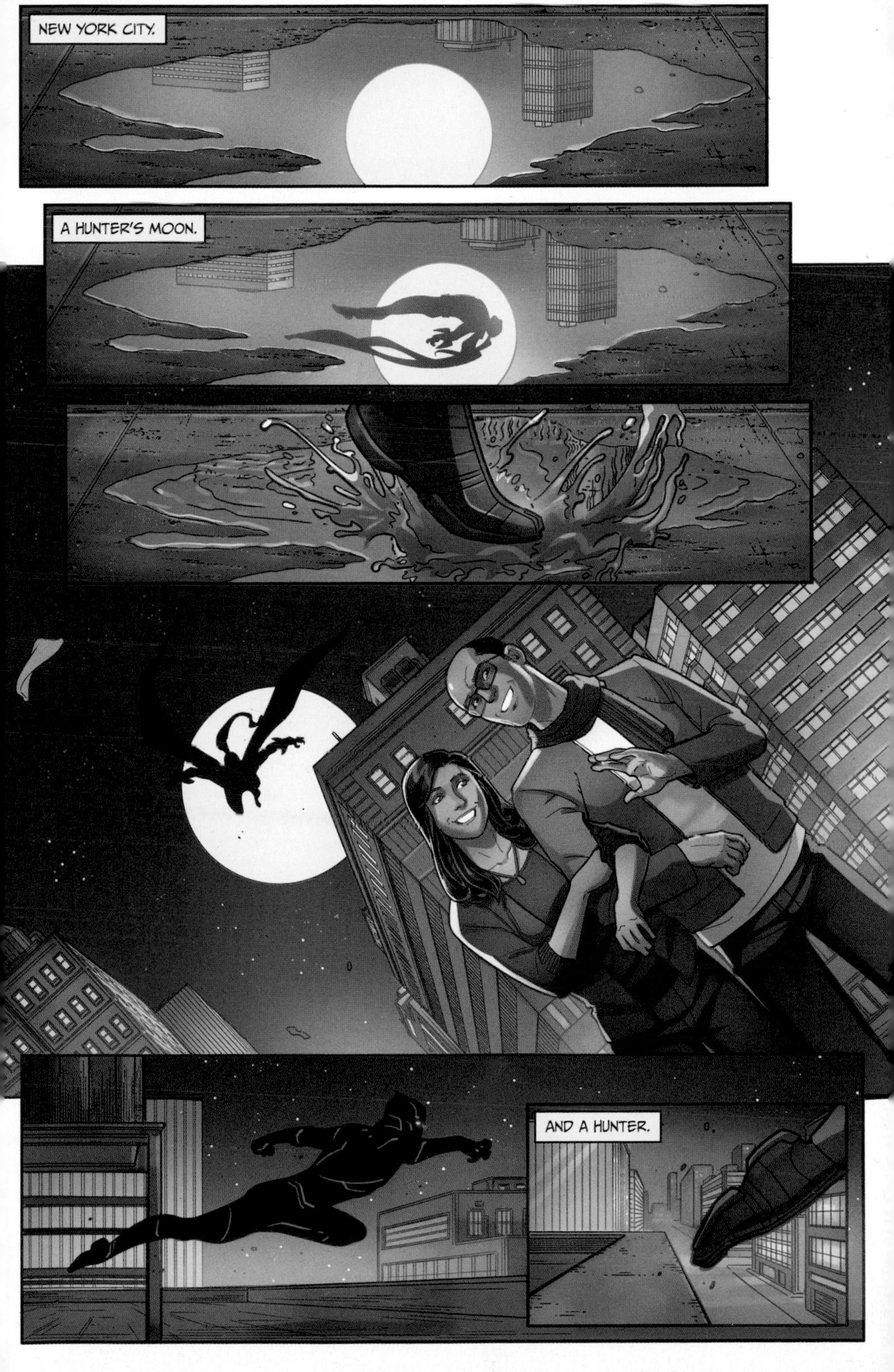
NEW YORK CITY.
A HUNTER'S MOON.
AND A HUNTER.

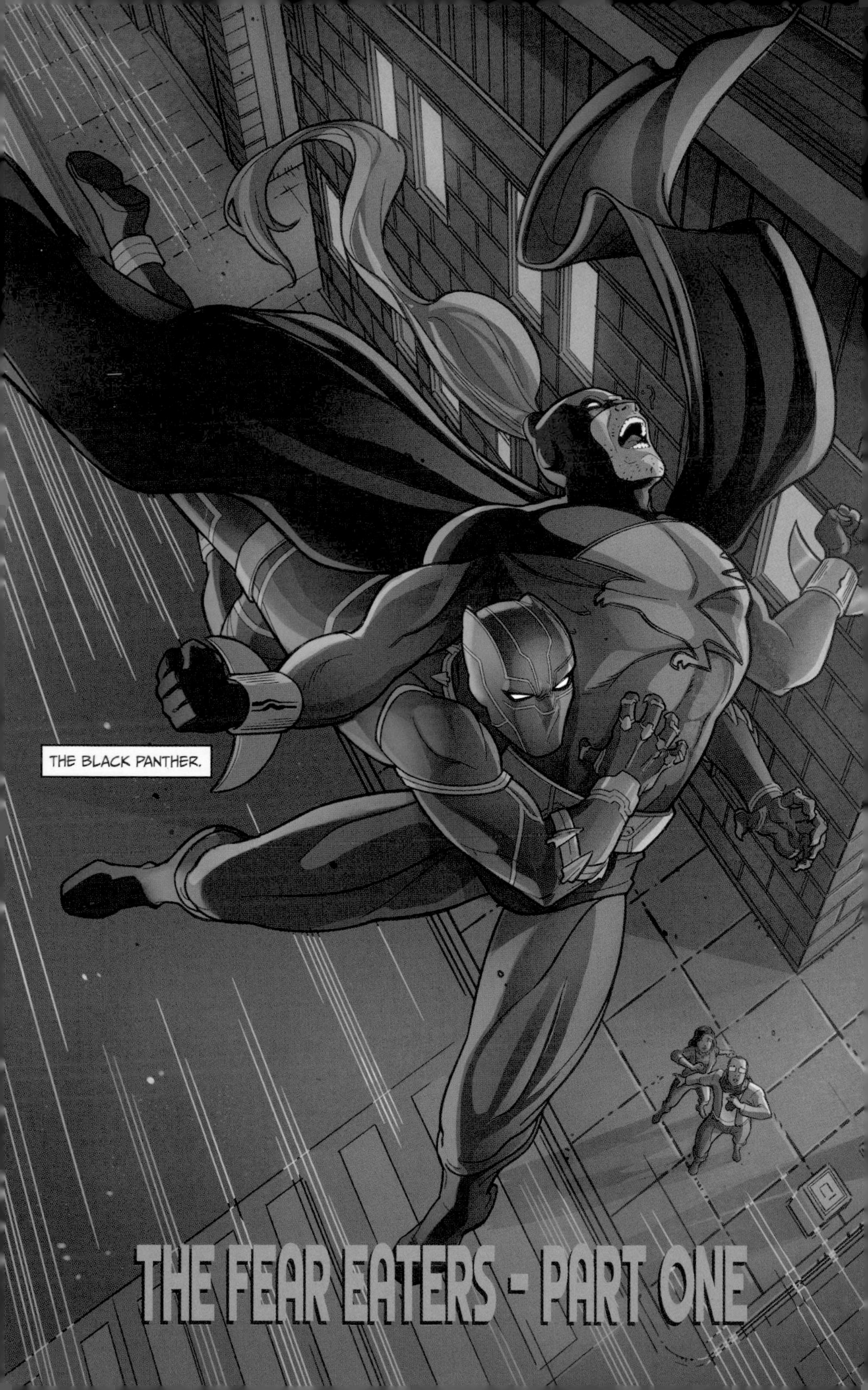
THE BLACK PANTHER.
THE FEAR EATERS - PART ONE

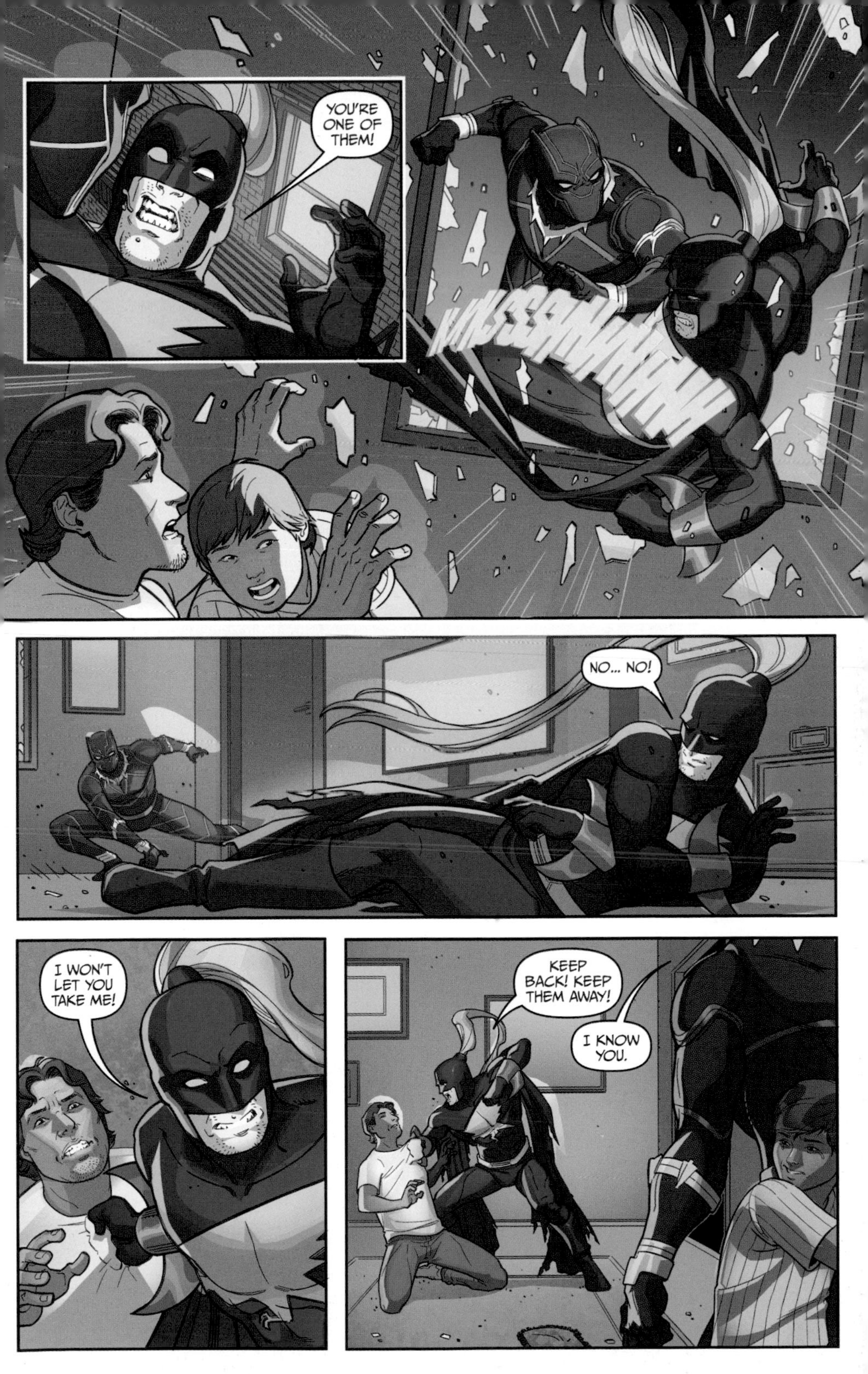
YOU'RE ONE OF THEM!
NO... NO!
I WON'T LET YOU TAKE ME!
KEEP BACK! KEEP THEM AWAY!
I KNOW YOU.

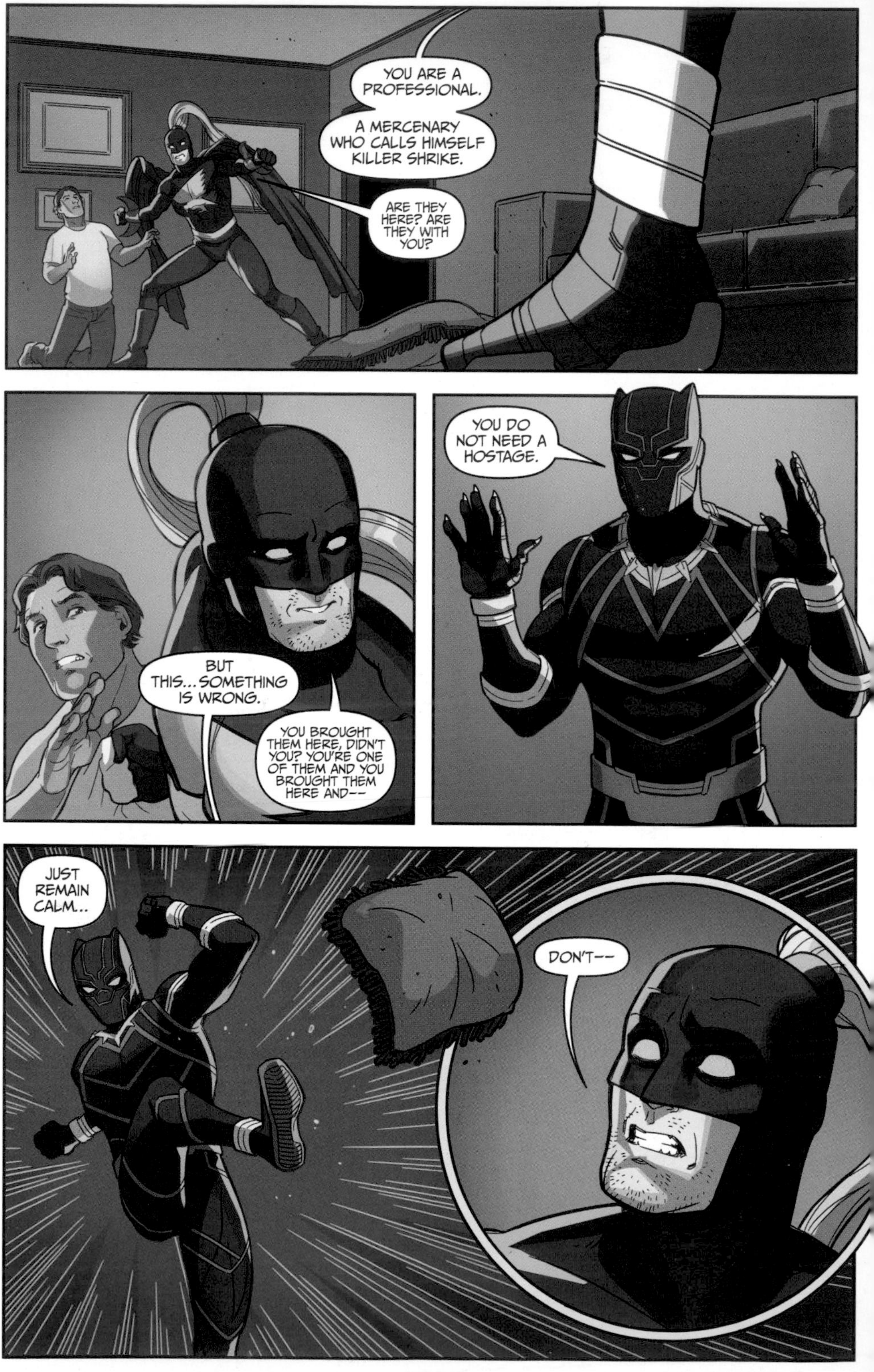
YOU ARE A PROFESSIONAL.
A MERCENARY WHO CALLS HIMSELF KILLER SHRIKE.
ARE THEY HERE? ARE THEY WITH YOU?
BUT THIS... SOMETHING IS WRONG.
YOU BROUGHT THEM HERE, DIDN'T YOU? YOU'RE ONE OF THEM AND YOU BROUGHT THEM HERE AND--
YOU DO NOT NEED A HOSTAGE.
JUST REMAIN CALM..
DON'T--

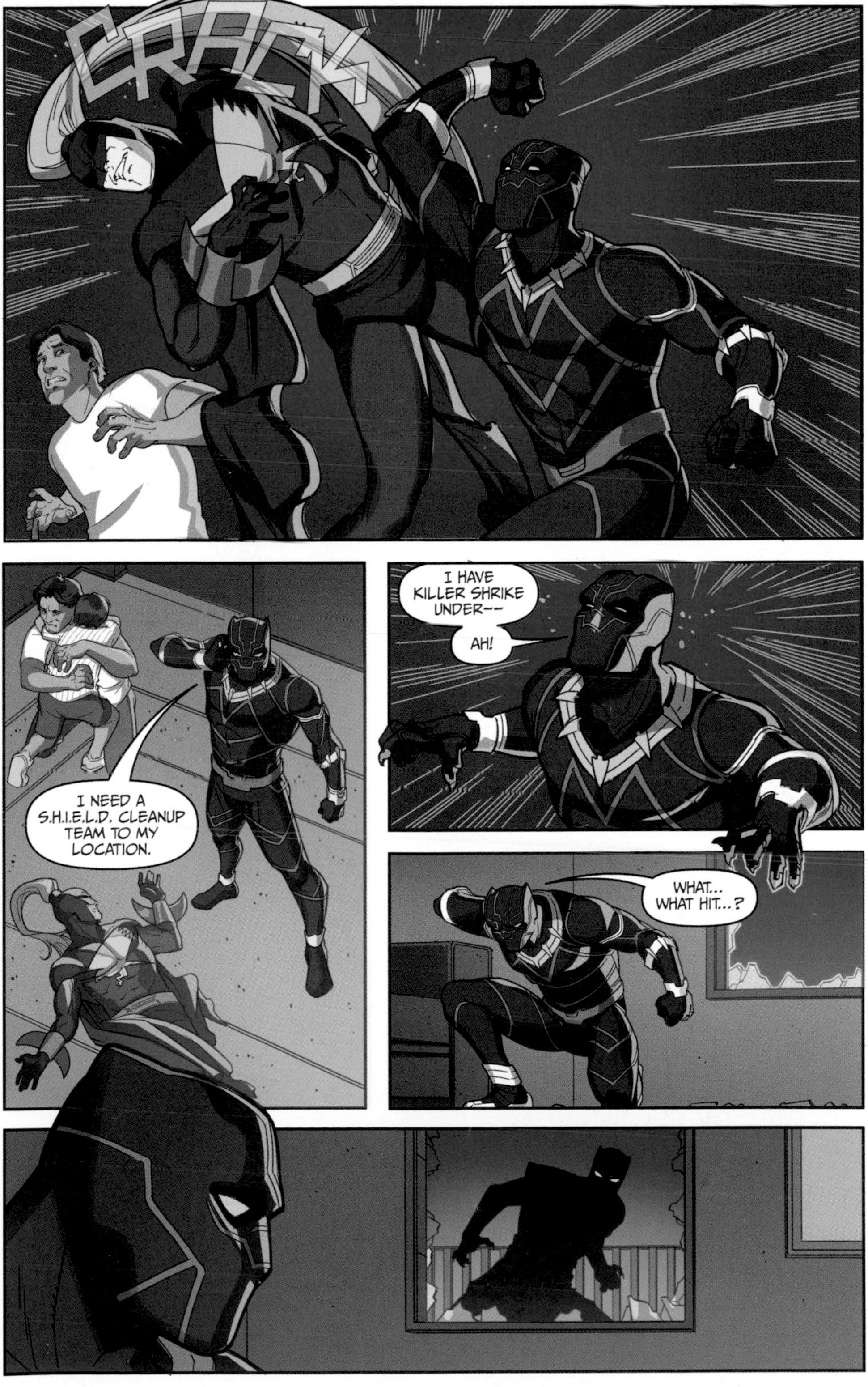
CRACK
I NEED A S.H.I.E.L.D. CLEANUP TEAM TO MY LOCATION.
I HAVE KILLER SHRIKE UNDER--
AH!
WHAT... WHAT HIT...?

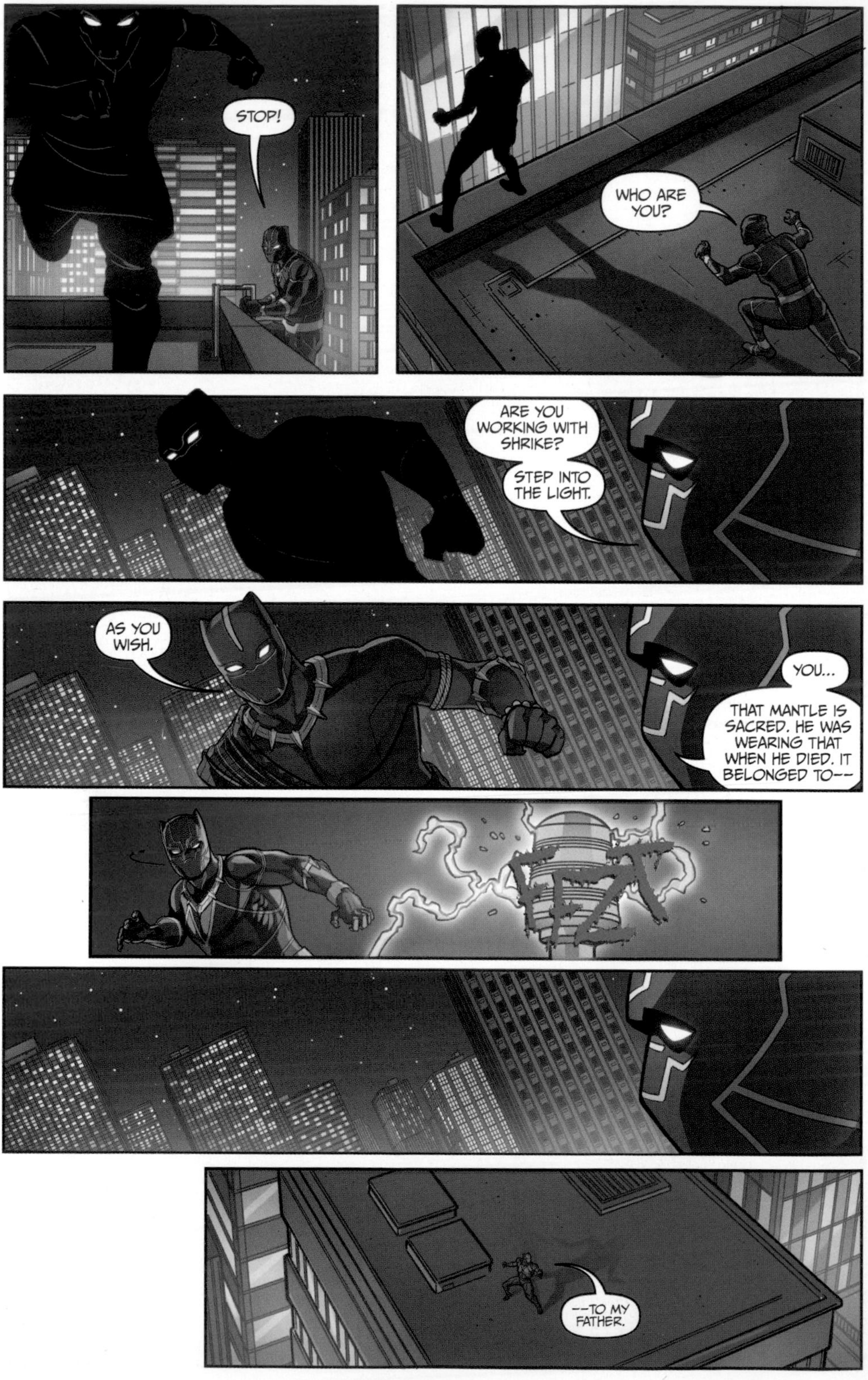
STOP!
WHO ARE YOU?
ARE YOU WORKING WITH SHRIKE?
STEP INTO THE LIGHT.
AS YOU WISH.
YOU...
THAT MANTLE IS SACRED. HE WAS WEARING THAT WHEN HE DIED. IT BELONGED TO--
FFZT
--TO MY FATHER.

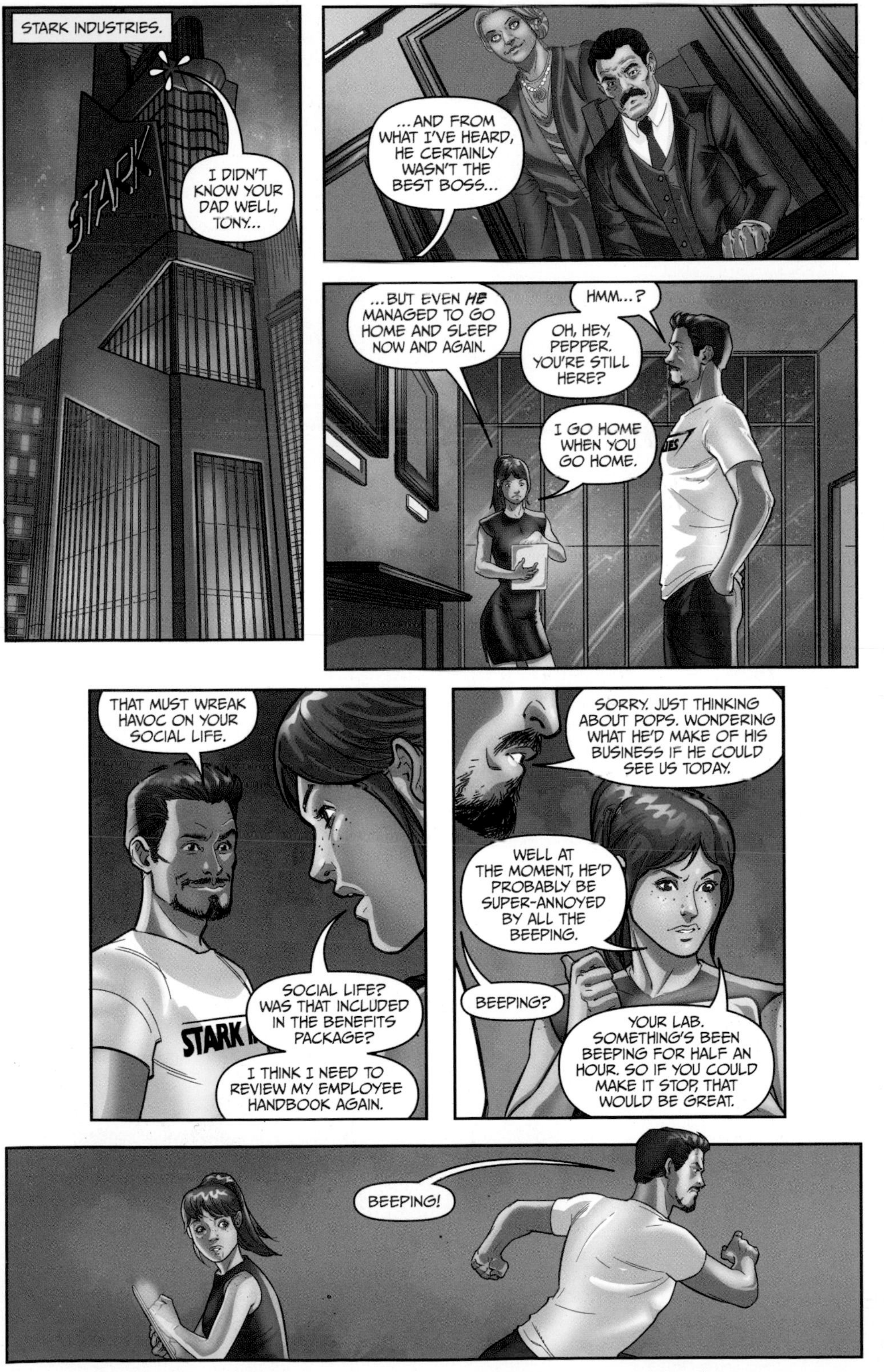
STARK INDUSTRIES.
STARK
I DIDN'T KNOW YOUR DAD WELL, TONY...
...AND FROM WHAT I'VE HEARD, HE CERTAINLY WASN'T THE BEST BOSS...
...BUT EVEN HE MANAGED TO GO HOME AND SLEEP NOW AND AGAIN.
HMM...?
OH, HEY, PEPPER. YOU'RE STILL HERE?
I GO HOME WHEN YOU GO HOME.
THAT MUST WREAK HAVOC ON YOUR SOCIAL LIFE.
SOCIAL LIFE? WAS THAT INCLUDED IN THE BENEFITS PACKAGE?
I THINK I NEED TO REVIEW MY EMPLOYEE HANDBOOK AGAIN.
SORRY. JUST THINKING ABOUT POPS. WONDERING WHAT HE'D MAKE OF HIS BUSINESS IF HE COULD SEE US TODAY.
WELL AT THE MOMENT, HE'D PROBABLY BE SUPER-ANNOYED BY ALL THE BEEPING.
BEEPING?
YOUR LAB. SOMETHING'S BEEN BEEPING FOR HALF AN HOUR. SO IF YOU COULD MAKE IT STOP, THAT WOULD BE GREAT.
BEEPING!

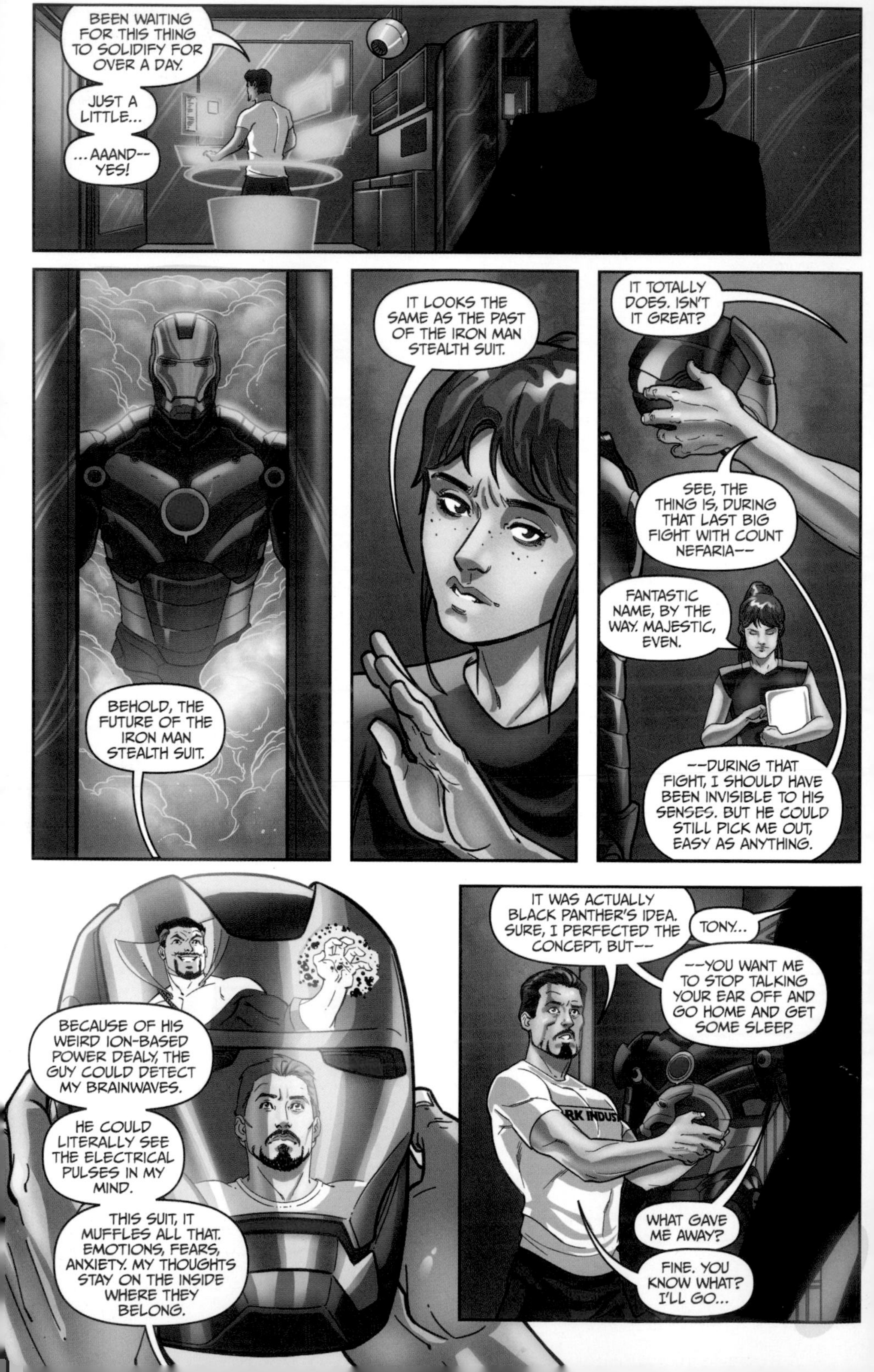
BEEN WAITING FOR THIS THING TO SOLIDIFY FOR OVER A DAY.
JUST A LITTLE...
...AAAND-- YES!
BEHOLD, THE FUTURE OF THE IRON MAN STEALTH SUIT.
IT LOOKS THE SAME AS THE PAST OF THE IRON MAN STEALTH SUIT.
IT TOTALLY DOES. ISN'T IT GREAT?
SEE, THE THING IS, DURING THAT LAST BIG FIGHT WITH COUNT NEFARIA--
FANTASTIC NAME, BY THE WAY. MAJESTIC, EVEN.
--DURING THAT FIGHT, I SHOULD HAVE BEEN INVISIBLE TO HIS SENSES. BUT HE COULD STILL PICK ME OUT, EASY AS ANYTHING.
BECAUSE OF HIS WEIRD ION-BASED POWER DEALY, THE GUY COULD DETECT MY BRAINWAVES.
HE COULD LITERALLY SEE THE ELECTRICAL PULSES IN MY MIND.
THIS SUIT, IT MUFFLES ALL THAT. EMOTIONS, FEARS, ANXIETY. MY THOUGHTS STAY ON THE INSIDE WHERE THEY BELONG.
IT WAS ACTUALLY BLACK PANTHER'S IDEA. SURE, I PERFECTED THE CONCEPT, BUT--
TONY...
--YOU WANT ME TO STOP TALKING YOUR EAR OFF AND GO HOME AND GET SOME SLEEP.
WHAT GAVE ME AWAY?
FINE. YOU KNOW WHAT? I'LL GO...

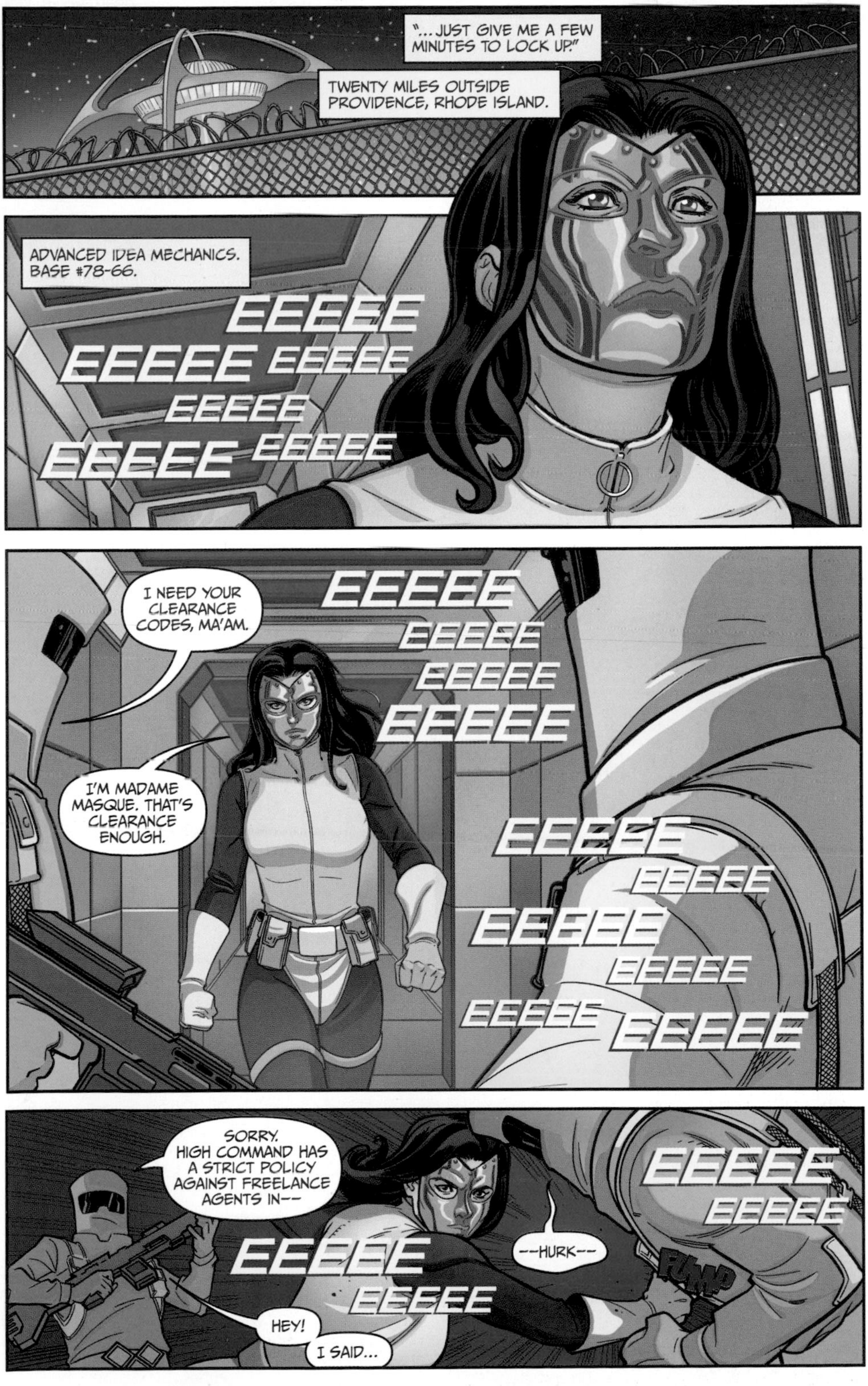
"... JUST GIVE ME A FEW MINUTES TO LOCK UP."
TWENTY MILES OUTSIDE PROVIDENCE, RHODE ISLAND.
ADVANCED IDEA MECHANICS. BASE #78-66.
EEEEE
EEEEE EEEEE
EEEEE
EEEEE EEEEE
I NEED YOUR CLEARANCE CODES, MA'AM.
EEEEE
EEEEE
EEEEE
EEEEE
I'M MADAME MASQUE. THAT'S CLEARANCE ENOUGH.
EEEEE
EEEEE
EEEEE
EEEEE
EEEEE EEEEE
SORRY. HIGH COMMAND HAS A STRICT POLICY AGAINST FREELANCE AGENTS IN--
EEEEE
EEEEE
--HURK--
EEEEE
EEEEE
HEY!
I SAID...

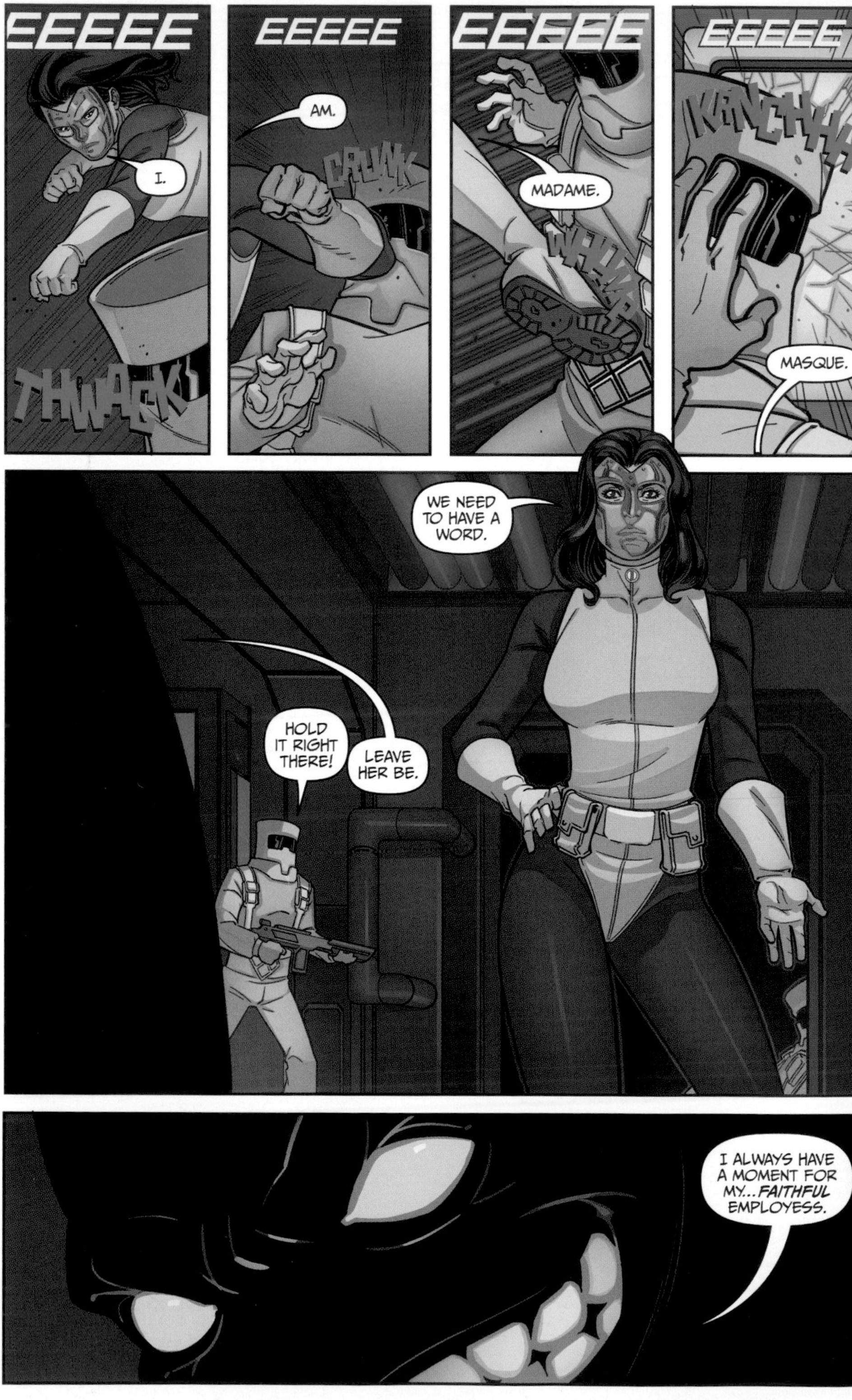
EEEEE
I.
THWACK!
EEEEE
AM.
CRUNK
EEEEE
MADAME.
WHUMP
EEEEE
KRNCHHH
MASQUE.
WE NEED TO HAVE A WORD.
HOLD IT RIGHT THERE!
LEAVE HER BE.
I ALWAYS HAVE A MOMENT FOR MY... *FAITHFUL* EMPLOYESS.

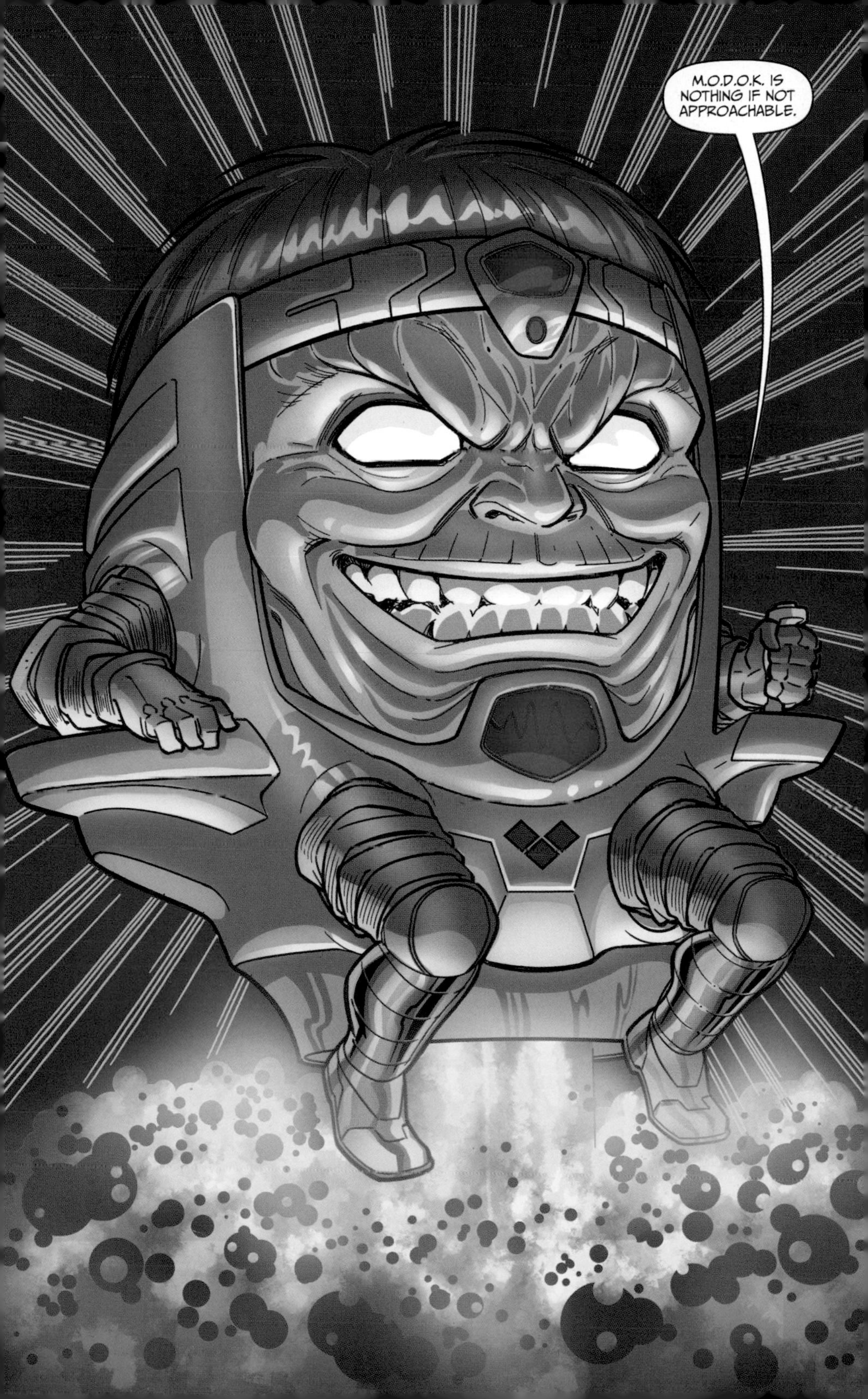
M.O.D.O.K. IS NOTHING IF NOT APPROACHABLE.

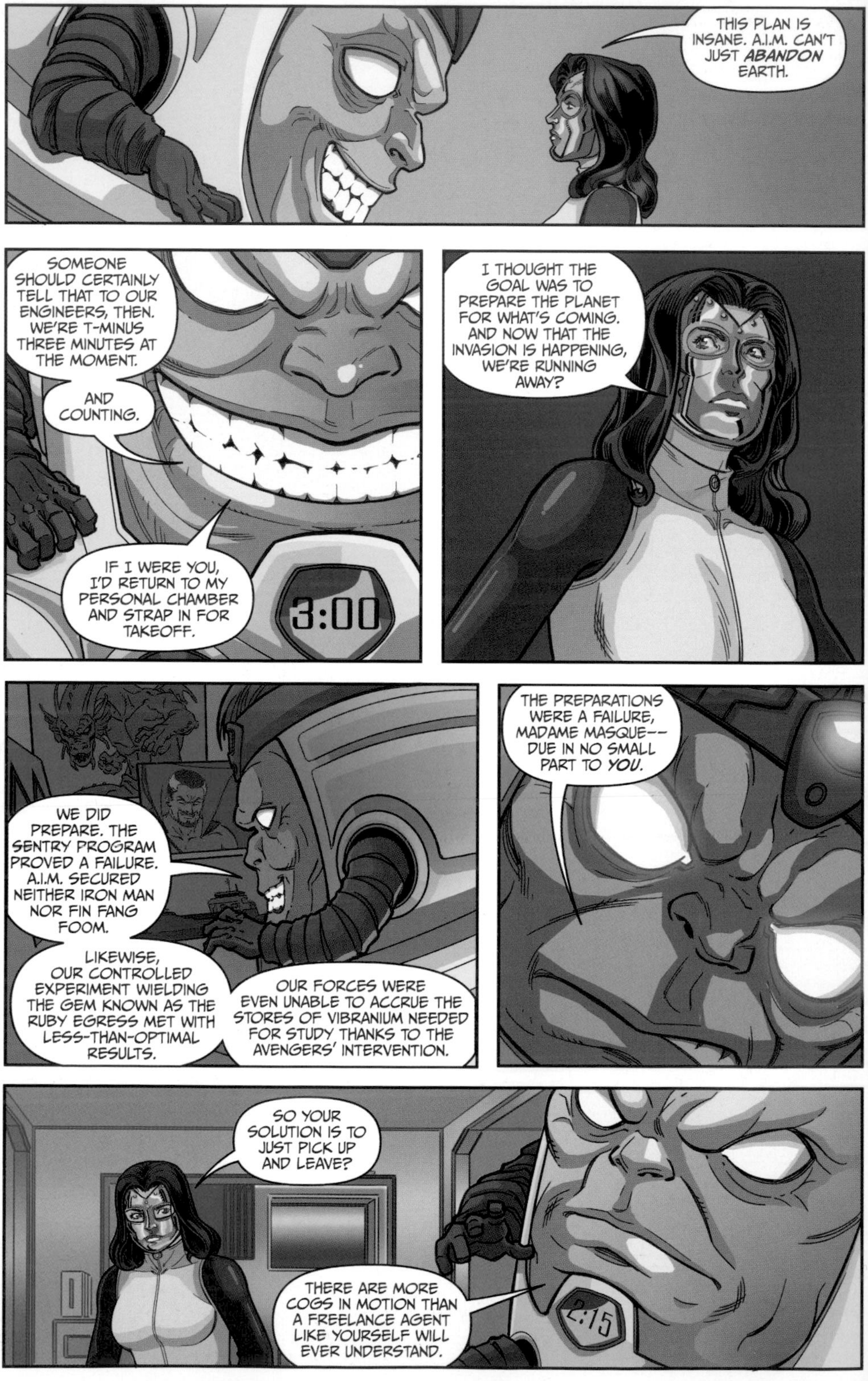
THIS PLAN IS INSANE. A.I.M. CAN'T JUST *ABANDON* EARTH.
SOMEONE SHOULD CERTAINLY TELL THAT TO OUR ENGINEERS, THEN. WE'RE T-MINUS THREE MINUTES AT THE MOMENT.
AND COUNTING.
IF I WERE YOU, I'D RETURN TO MY PERSONAL CHAMBER AND STRAP IN FOR TAKEOFF.
3:00
I THOUGHT THE GOAL WAS TO PREPARE THE PLANET FOR WHAT'S COMING. AND NOW THAT THE INVASION IS HAPPENING, WE'RE RUNNING AWAY?
WE DID PREPARE. THE SENTRY PROGRAM PROVED A FAILURE. A.I.M. SECURED NEITHER IRON MAN NOR FIN FANG FOOM.
LIKEWISE, OUR CONTROLLED EXPERIMENT WIELDING THE GEM KNOWN AS THE RUBY EGRESS MET WITH LESS-THAN-OPTIMAL RESULTS.
OUR FORCES WERE EVEN UNABLE TO ACCRUE THE STORES OF VIBRANIUM NEEDED FOR STUDY THANKS TO THE AVENGERS' INTERVENTION.
THE PREPARATIONS WERE A FAILURE, MADAME MASQUE-- DUE IN NO SMALL PART TO *YOU.*
SO YOUR SOLUTION IS TO JUST PICK UP AND LEAVE?
THERE ARE MORE COGS IN MOTION THAN A FREELANCE AGENT LIKE YOURSELF WILL EVER UNDERSTAND.
2:15

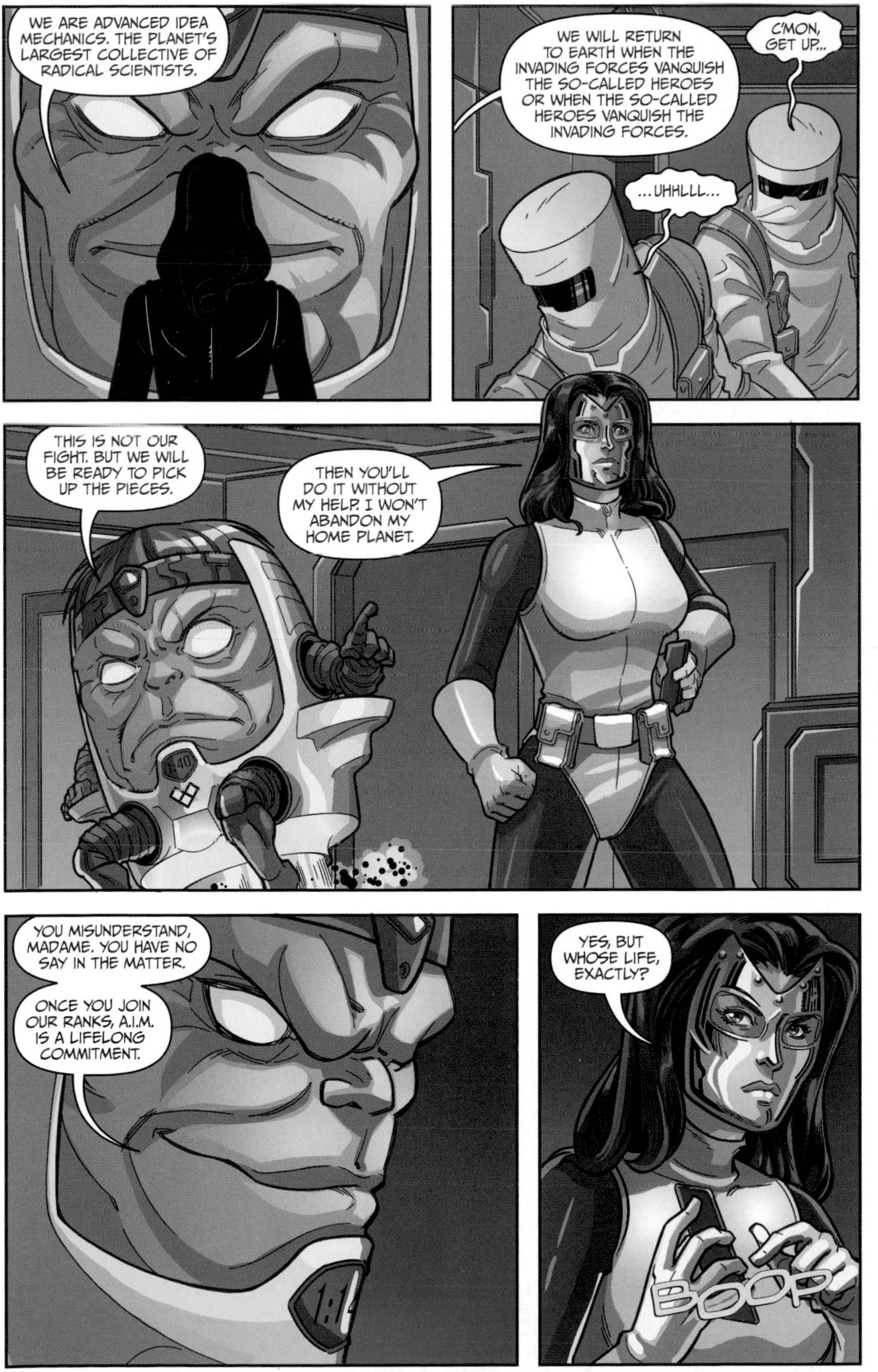
WE ARE ADVANCED IDEA MECHANICS. THE PLANET'S LARGEST COLLECTIVE OF RADICAL SCIENTISTS.
WE WILL RETURN TO EARTH WHEN THE INVADING FORCES VANQUISH THE SO-CALLED HEROES OR WHEN THE SO-CALLED HEROES VANQUISH THE INVADING FORCES.
C'MON, GET UP...
...UHHLLL...
THIS IS NOT OUR FIGHT. BUT WE WILL BE READY TO PICK UP THE PIECES.
THEN YOU'LL DO IT WITHOUT MY HELP. I WON'T ABANDON MY HOME PLANET.
YOU MISUNDERSTAND, MADAME. YOU HAVE NO SAY IN THE MATTER.
ONCE YOU JOIN OUR RANKS, A.I.M. IS A LIFELONG COMMITMENT.
YES, BUT WHOSE LIFE, EXACTLY?
BOOP

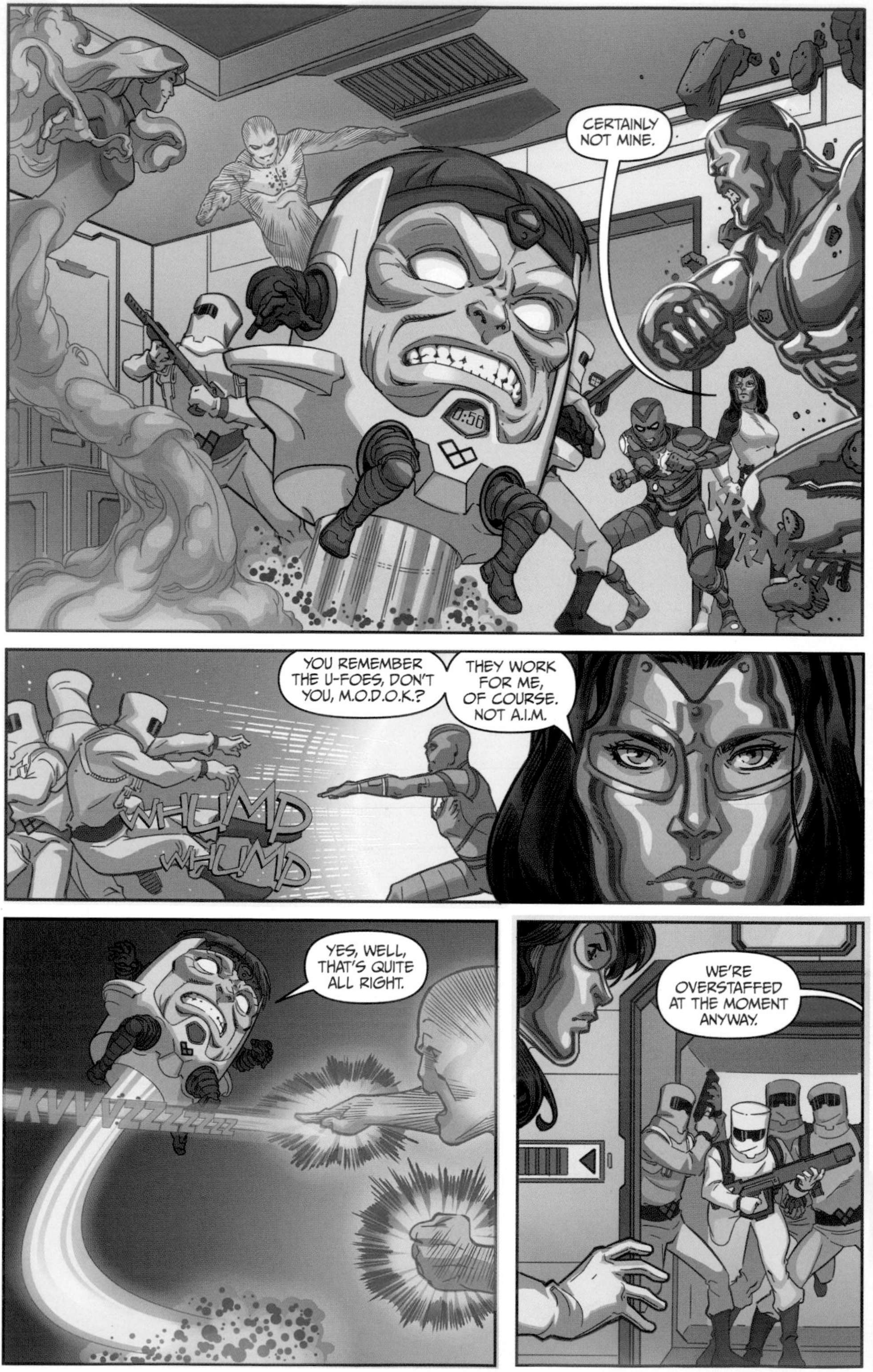
CERTAINLY NOT MINE.
YOU REMEMBER THE U-FOES, DON'T YOU, M.O.D.O.K.?
THEY WORK FOR ME, OF COURSE. NOT A.I.M.
WHUMP
WHUMP
YES, WELL, THAT'S QUITE ALL RIGHT.
WE'RE OVERSTAFFED AT THE MOMENT ANYWAY.

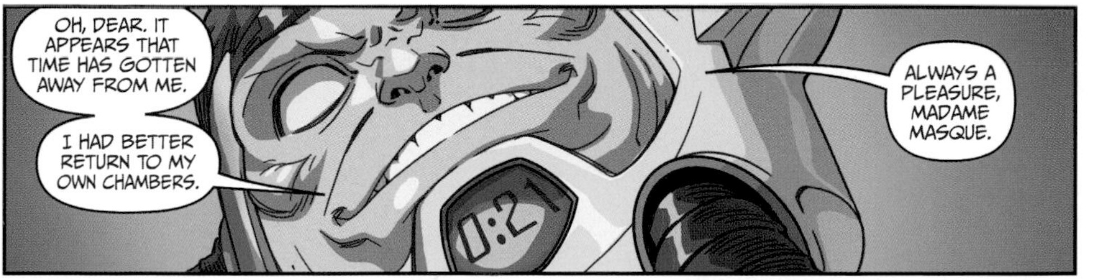
OH, DEAR. IT APPEARS THAT TIME HAS GOTTEN AWAY FROM ME.
I HAD BETTER RETURN TO MY OWN CHAMBERS.
ALWAYS A PLEASURE, MADAME MASQUE.
0:21

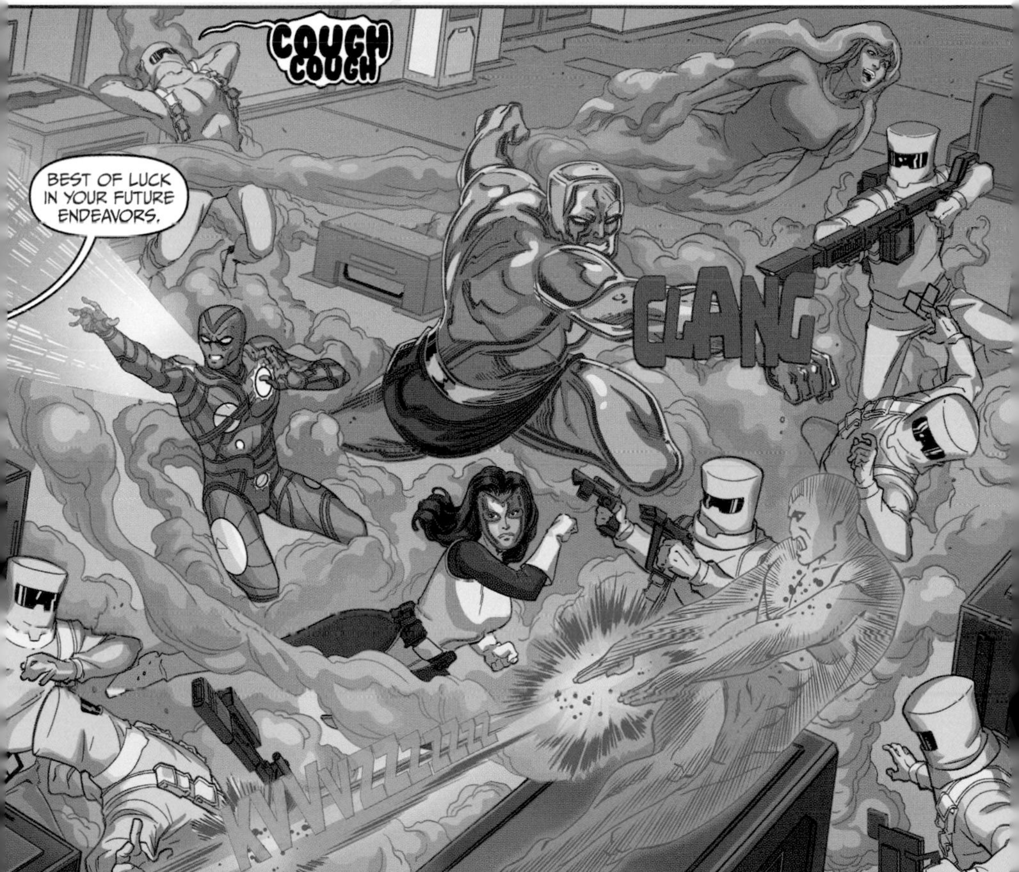
COUGH COUGH
BEST OF LUCK IN YOUR FUTURE ENDEAVORS.
CLANG
KVVVZZZZZZZ

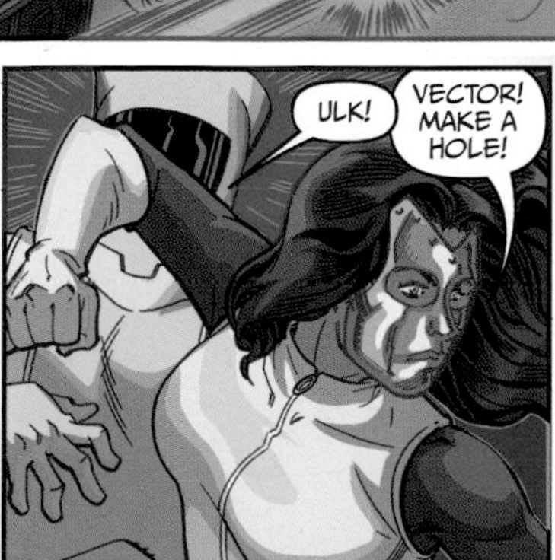
ULK!
VECTOR! MAKE A HOLE!

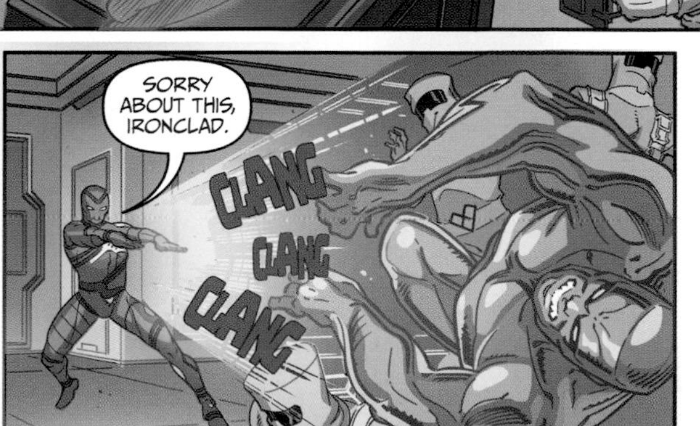
SORRY ABOUT THIS, IRONCLAD.
CLANG
CLANG
CLANG

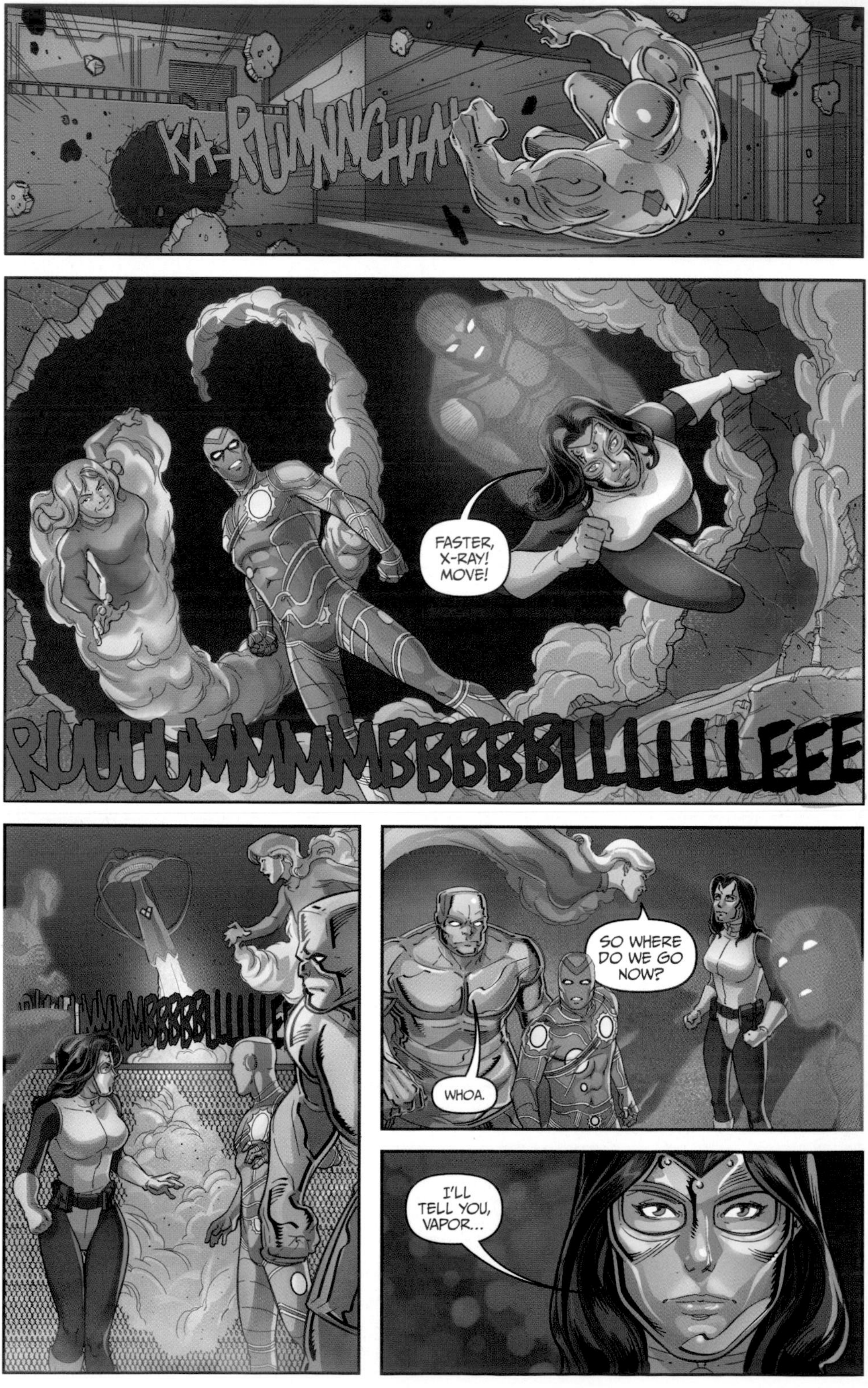
KA-RUNNNCHH
FASTER, X-RAY! MOVE!
RUUUMMMMBBBBBLLLLLLEEE
SO WHERE DO WE GO NOW?
WHOA.
I'LL TELL YOU, VAPOR...

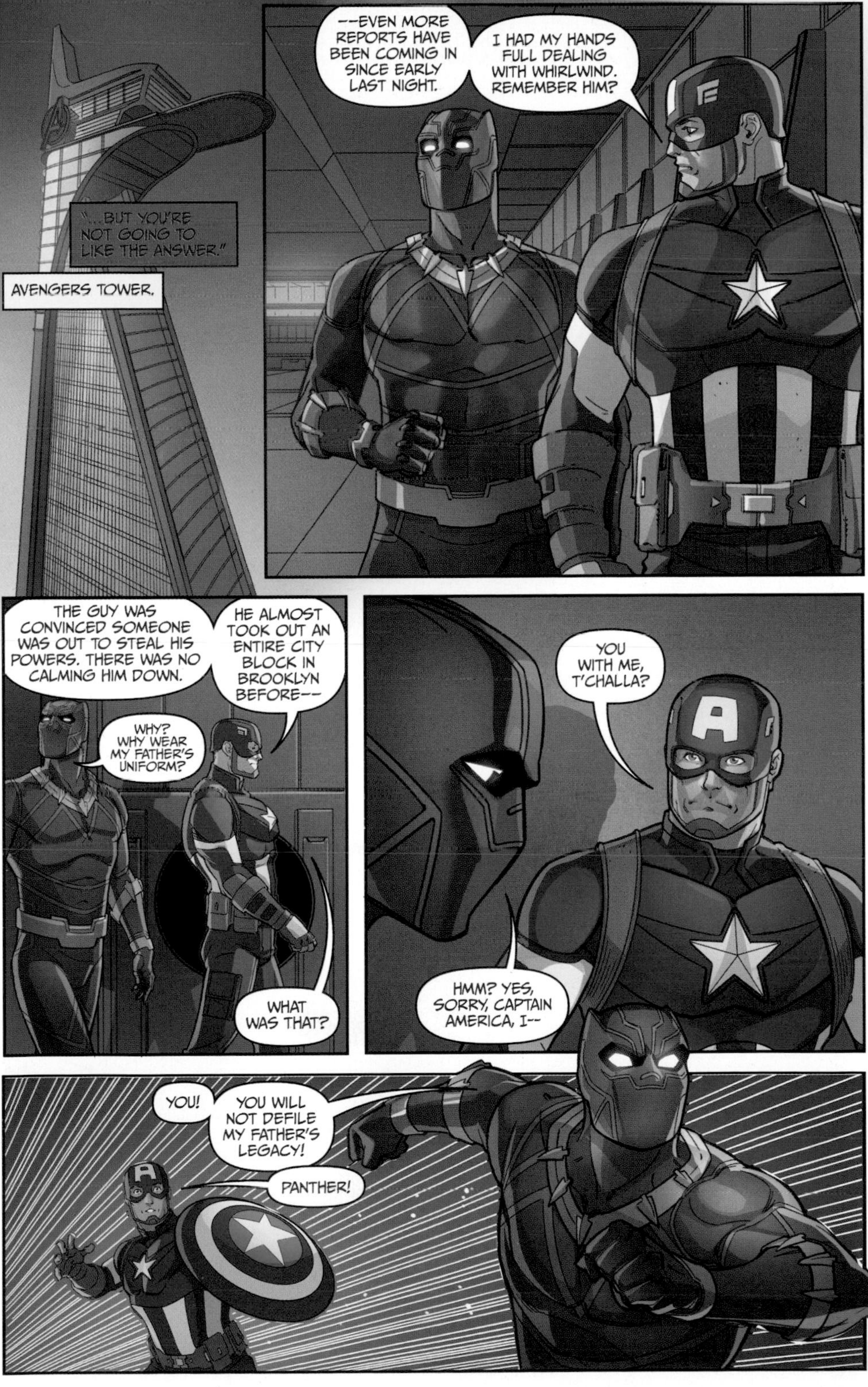
"...BUT YOU'RE NOT GOING TO LIKE THE ANSWER."
AVENGERS TOWER.
--EVEN MORE REPORTS HAVE BEEN COMING IN SINCE EARLY LAST NIGHT.
I HAD MY HANDS FULL DEALING WITH WHIRLWIND. REMEMBER HIM?
THE GUY WAS CONVINCED SOMEONE WAS OUT TO STEAL HIS POWERS. THERE WAS NO CALMING HIM DOWN.
HE ALMOST TOOK OUT AN ENTIRE CITY BLOCK IN BROOKLYN BEFORE--
WHY? WHY WEAR MY FATHER'S UNIFORM?
WHAT WAS THAT?
YOU WITH ME, T'CHALLA?
HMM? YES, SORRY, CAPTAIN AMERICA, I--
YOU!
YOU WILL NOT DEFILE MY FATHER'S LEGACY!
PANTHER!

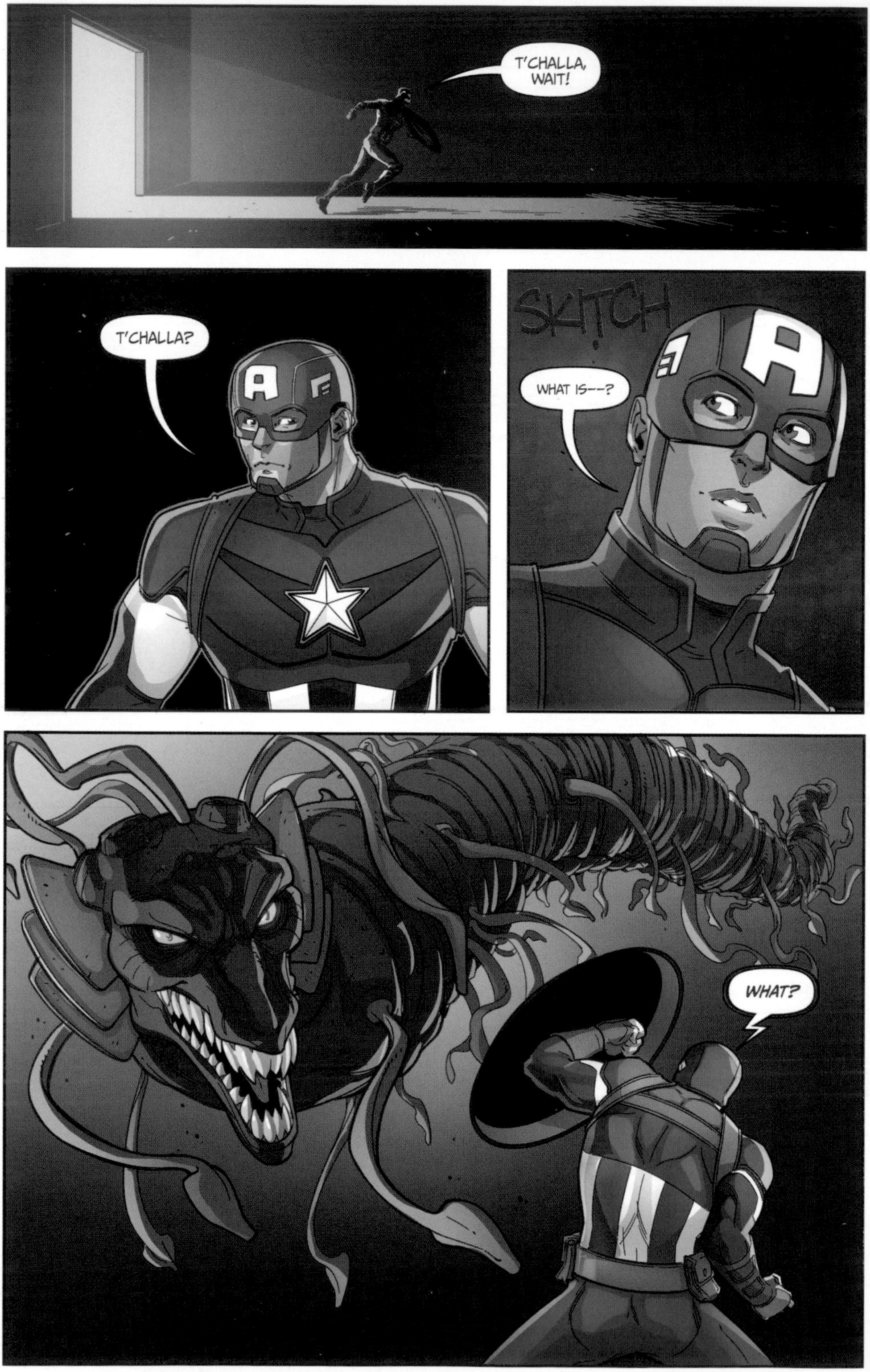
T'CHALLA, WAIT!
T'CHALLA?
SKITCH
WHAT IS--?
WHAT?

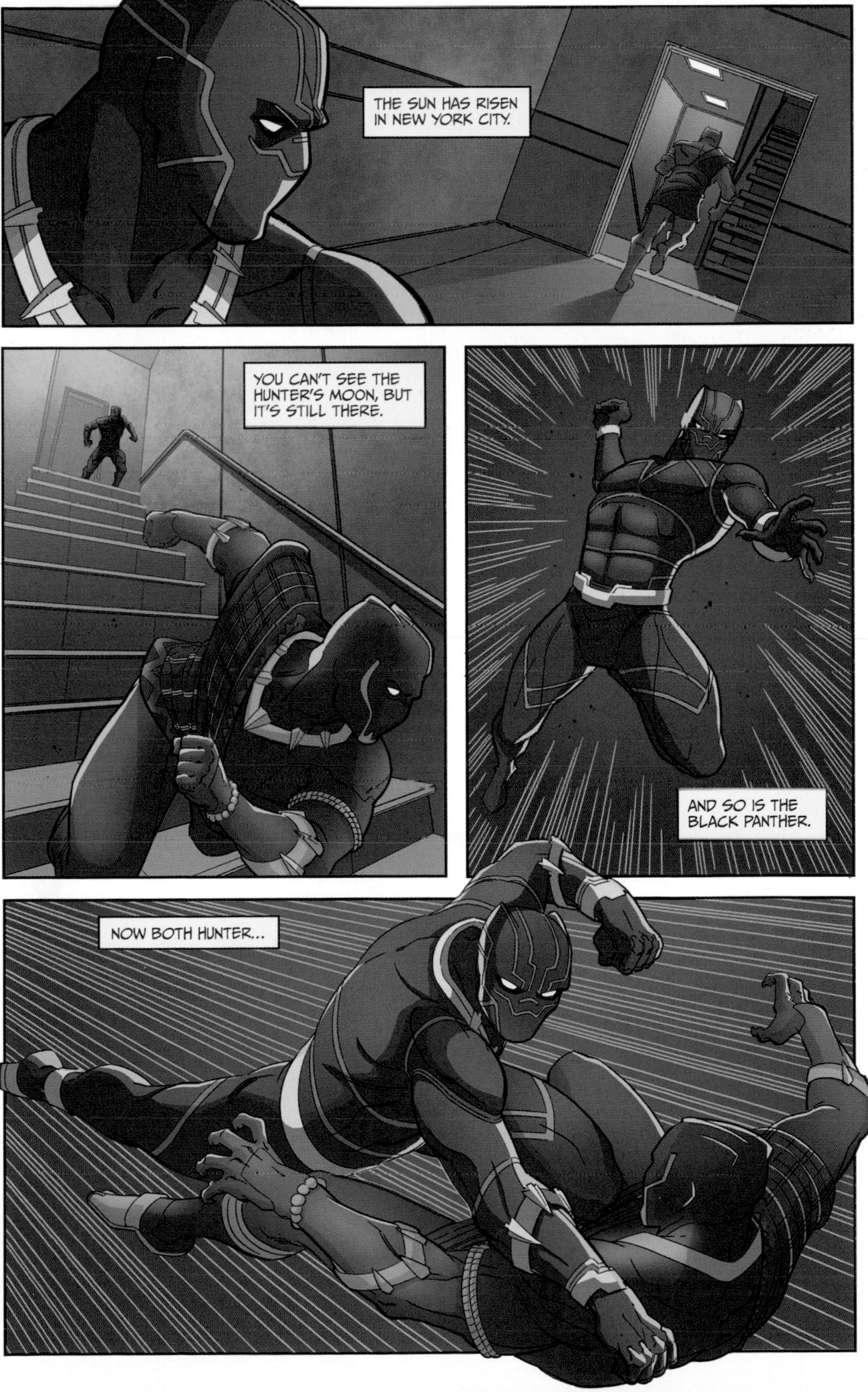
THE SUN HAS RISEN IN NEW YORK CITY.
YOU CAN'T SEE THE HUNTER'S MOON, BUT IT'S STILL THERE.
AND SO IS THE BLACK PANTHER.
NOW BOTH HUNTER...

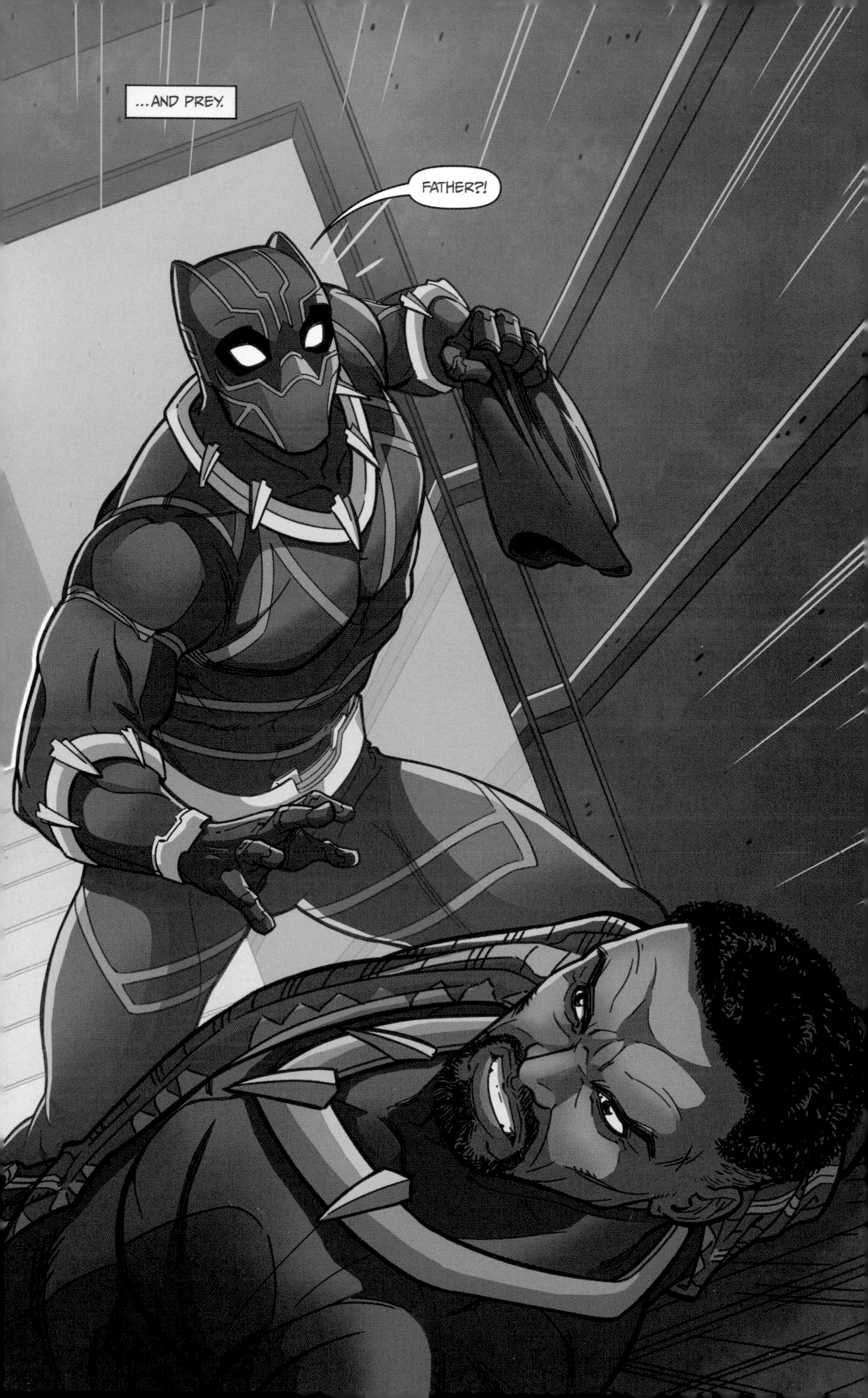
...AND PREY.
FATHER?!

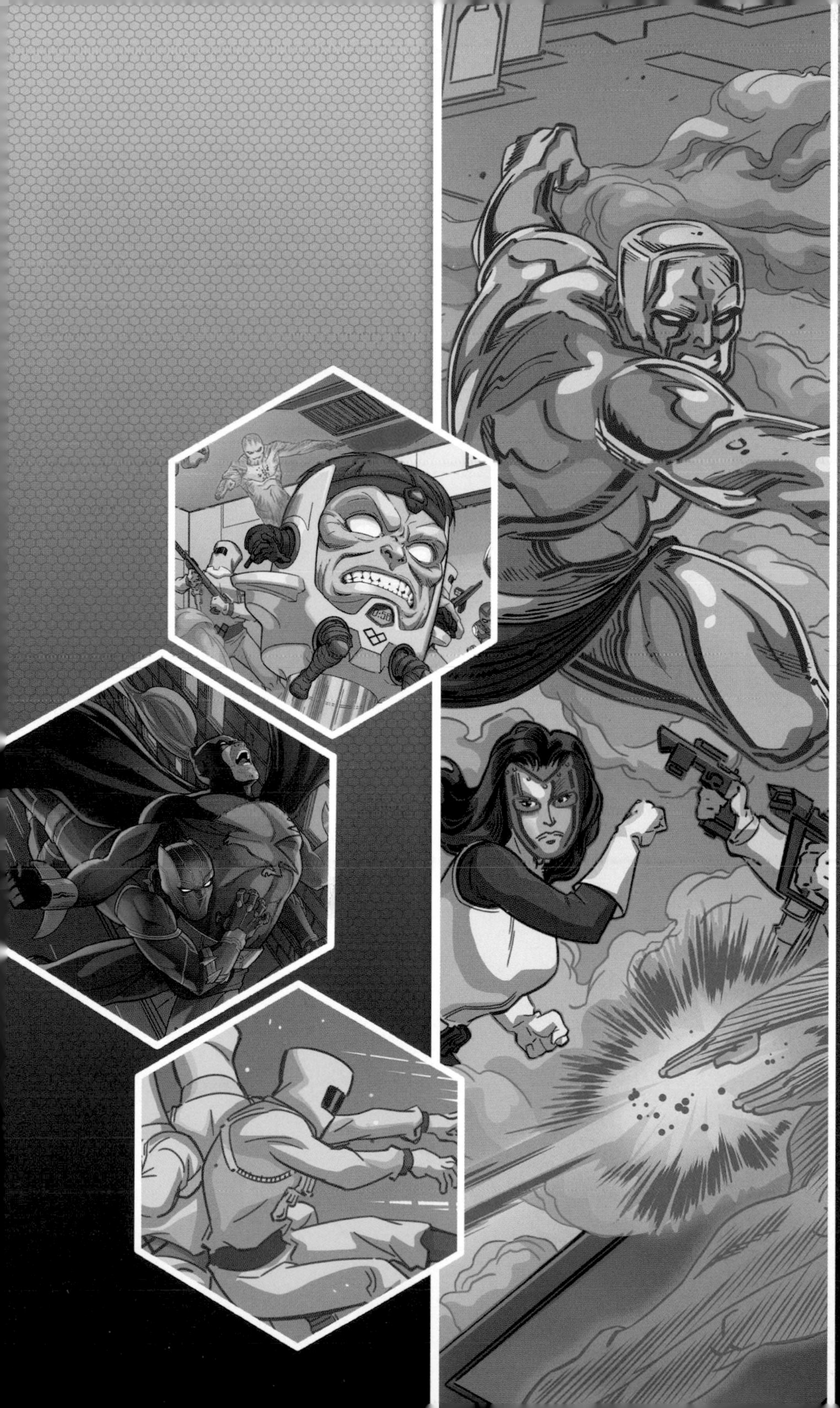

ART BY: JON SOMMARIVA
COLORS BY: PAC 23

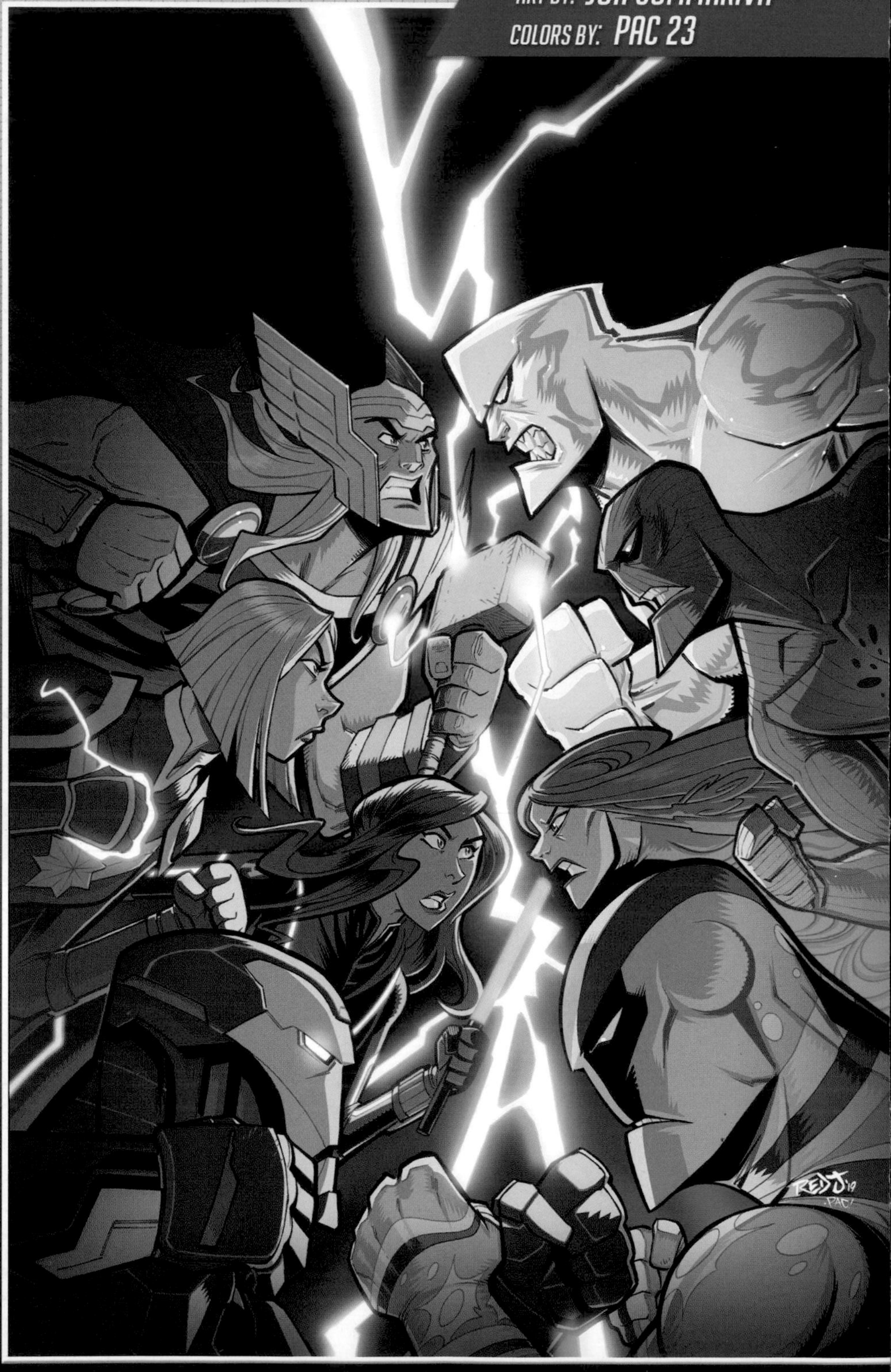

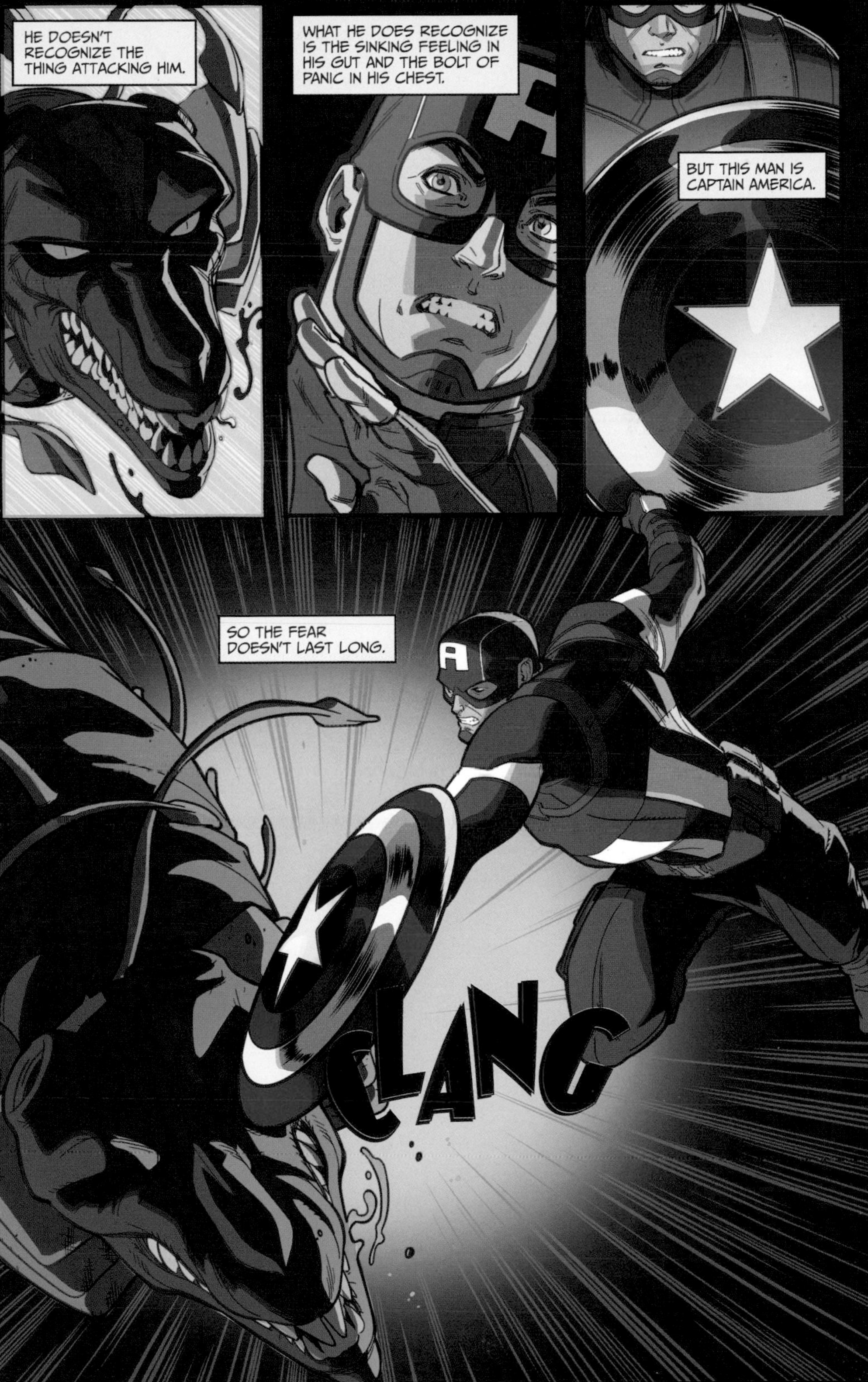
HE DOESN'T RECOGNIZE THE THING ATTACKING HIM.
WHAT HE DOES RECOGNIZE IS THE SINKING FEELING IN HIS GUT AND THE BOLT OF PANIC IN HIS CHEST.
BUT THIS MAN IS CAPTAIN AMERICA.
SO THE FEAR DOESN'T LAST LONG.
CLANG

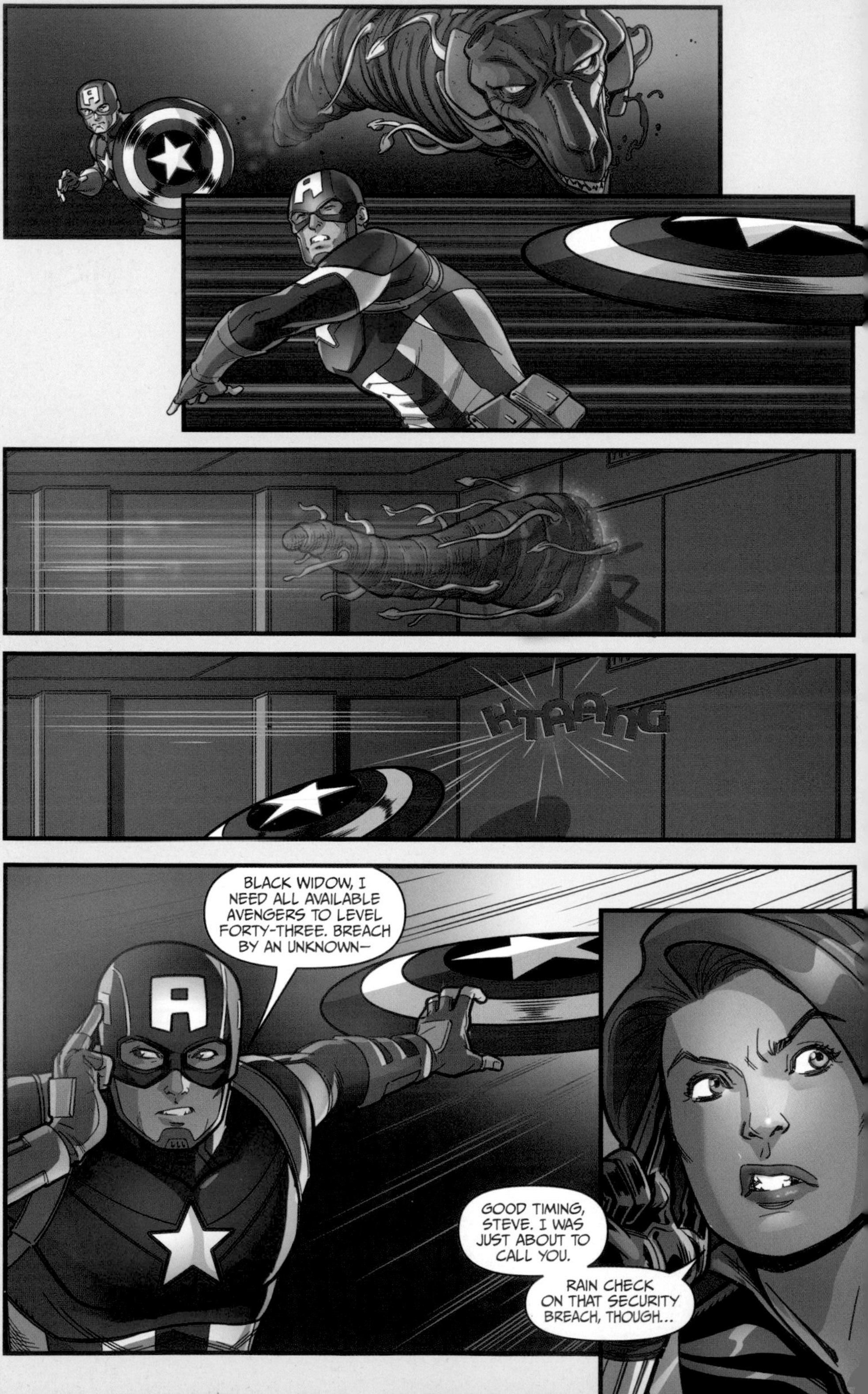
KTAAANG
BLACK WIDOW, I NEED ALL AVAILABLE AVENGERS TO LEVEL FORTY-THREE. BREACH BY AN UNKNOWN—
GOOD TIMING, STEVE. I WAS JUST ABOUT TO CALL YOU.
RAIN CHECK ON THAT SECURITY BREACH, THOUGH...

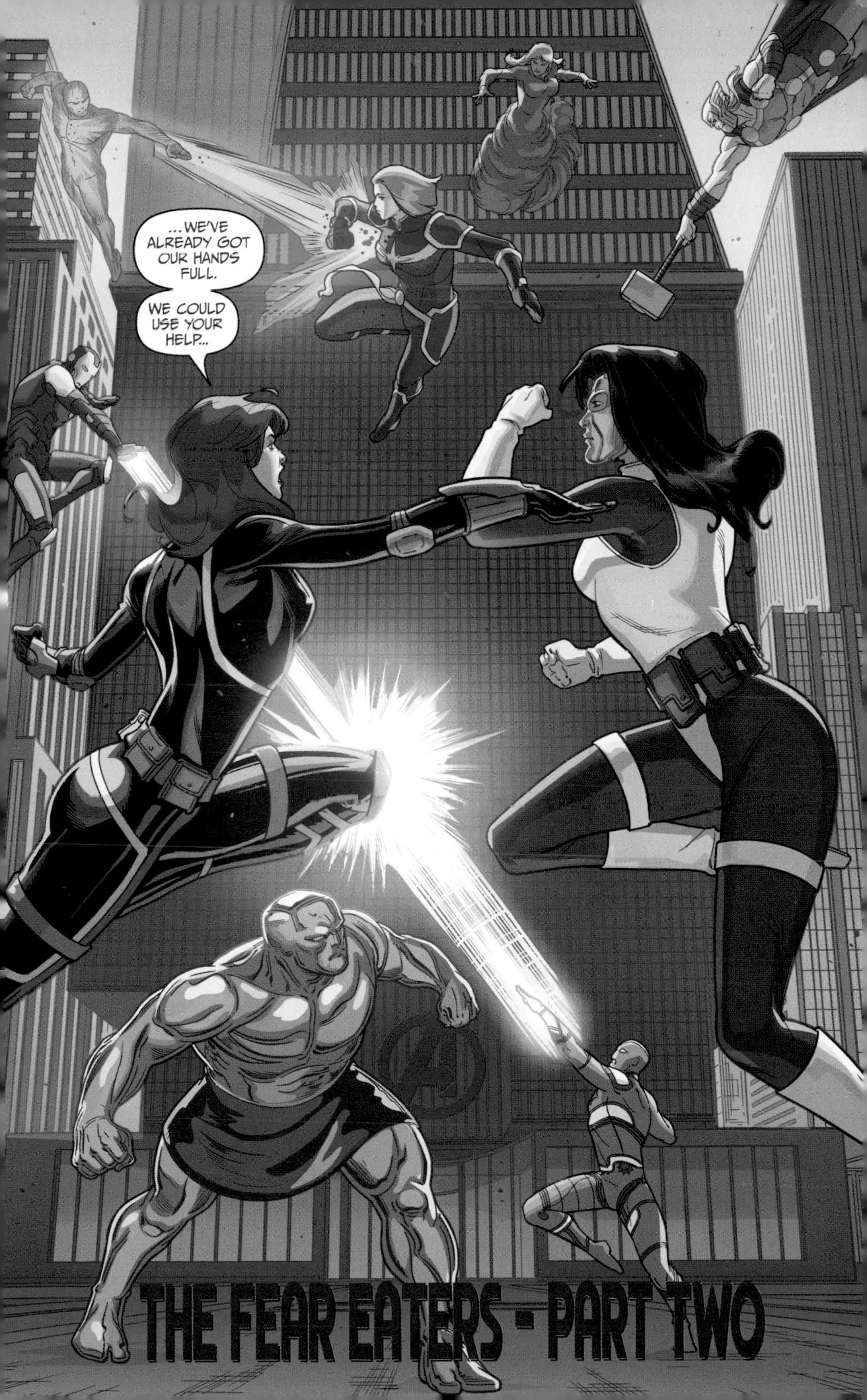
...WE'VE ALREADY GOT OUR HANDS FULL.
WE COULD USE YOUR HELP...
THE FEAR EATERS - PART TWO

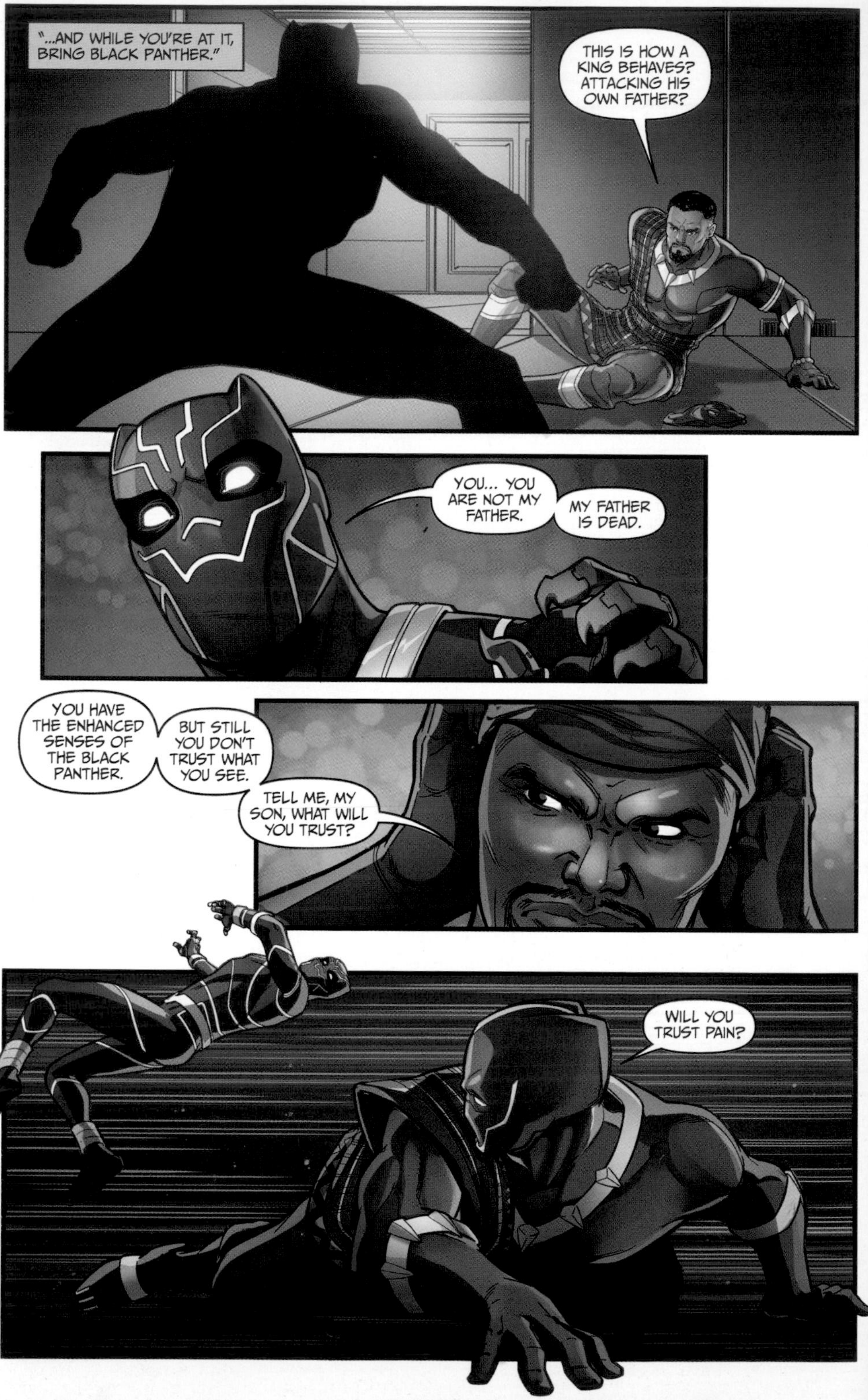
"...AND WHILE YOU'RE AT IT, BRING BLACK PANTHER."
THIS IS HOW A KING BEHAVES? ATTACKING HIS OWN FATHER?
YOU... YOU ARE NOT MY FATHER.
MY FATHER IS DEAD.
YOU HAVE THE ENHANCED SENSES OF THE BLACK PANTHER.
BUT STILL YOU DON'T TRUST WHAT YOU SEE.
TELL ME, MY SON, WHAT WILL YOU TRUST?
WILL YOU TRUST PAIN?

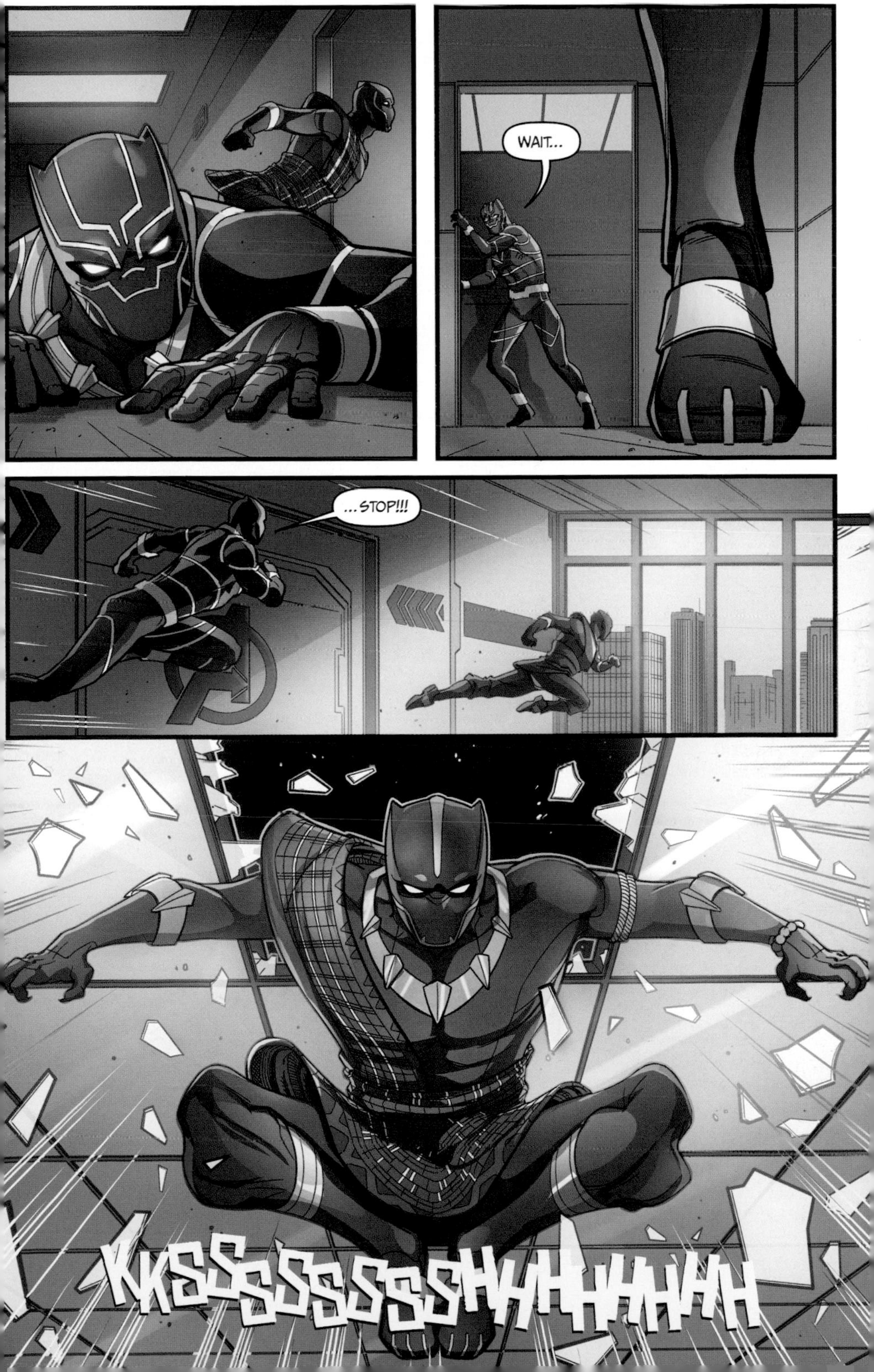
WAIT...
...STOP!!!
KKSSSSSSSSHHHHHHH

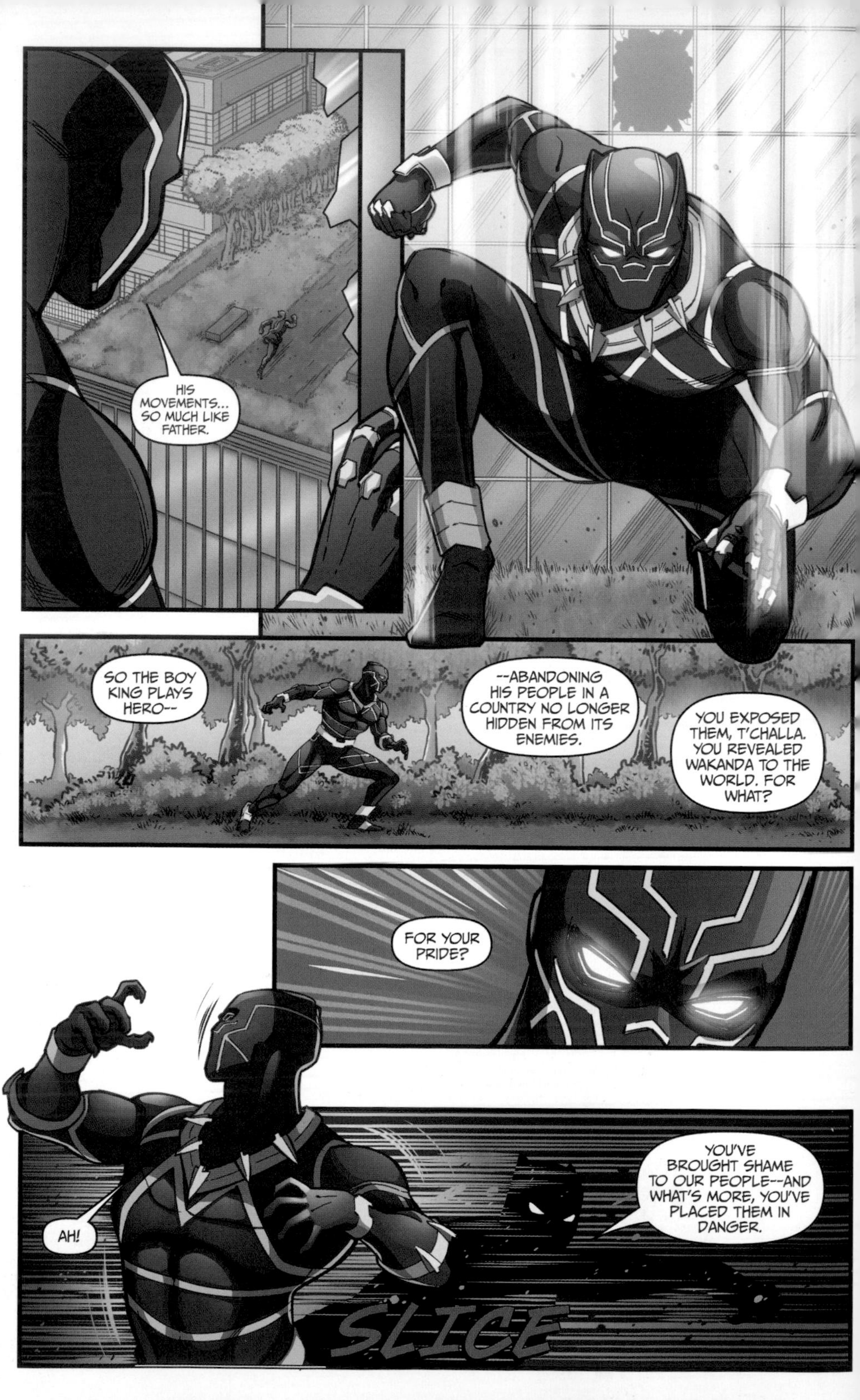
HIS MOVEMENTS... SO MUCH LIKE FATHER.
SO THE BOY KING PLAYS HERO--
--ABANDONING HIS PEOPLE IN A COUNTRY NO LONGER HIDDEN FROM ITS ENEMIES.
YOU EXPOSED THEM, T'CHALLA. YOU REVEALED WAKANDA TO THE WORLD. FOR WHAT?
FOR YOUR PRIDE?
YOU'VE BROUGHT SHAME TO OUR PEOPLE--AND WHAT'S MORE, YOU'VE PLACED THEM IN DANGER.
AH!
SLICE

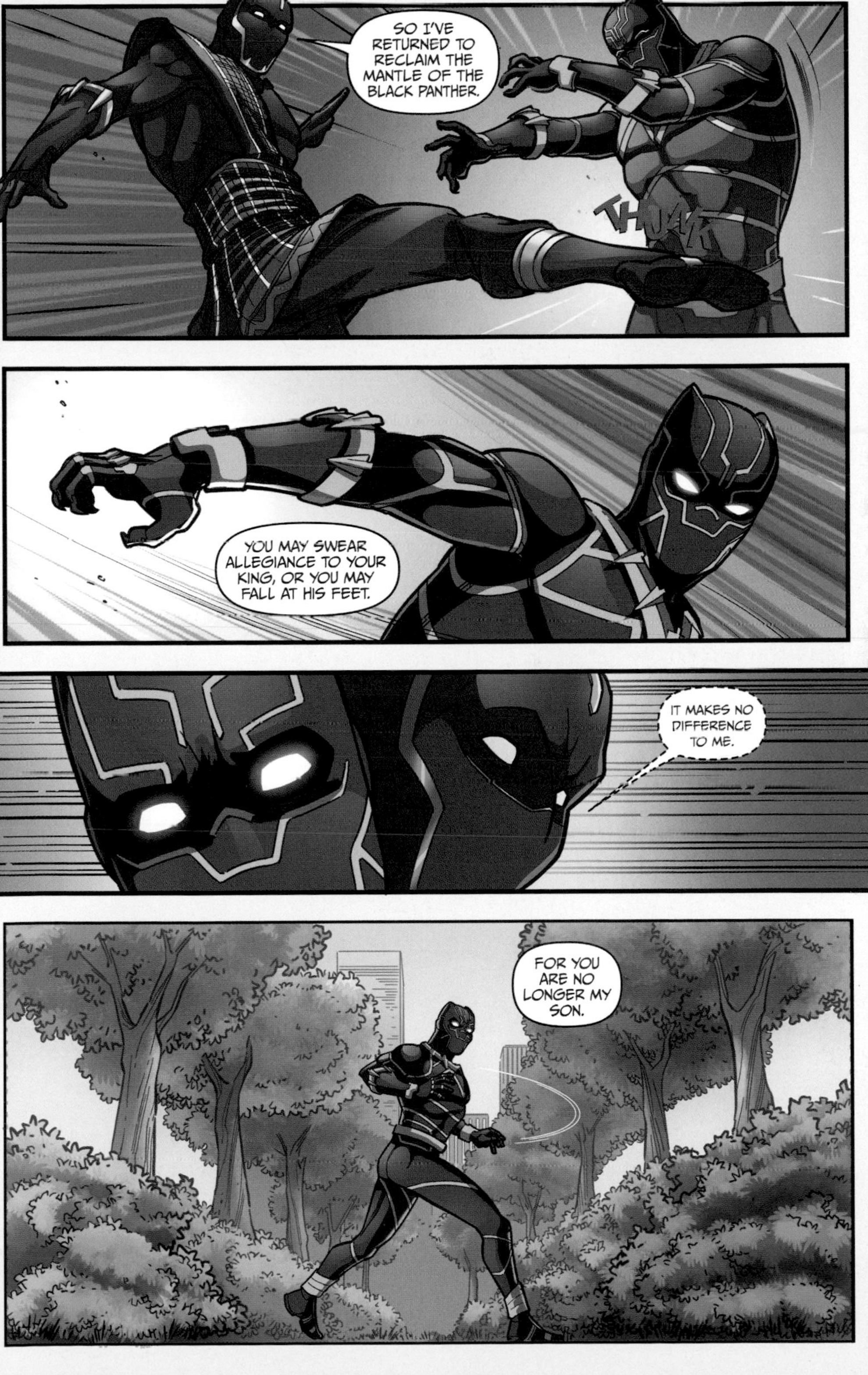
SO I'VE RETURNED TO RECLAIM THE MANTLE OF THE BLACK PANTHER.
THWAK
YOU MAY SWEAR ALLEGIANCE TO YOUR KING, OR YOU MAY FALL AT HIS FEET.
IT MAKES NO DIFFERENCE TO ME.
FOR YOU ARE NO LONGER MY SON.

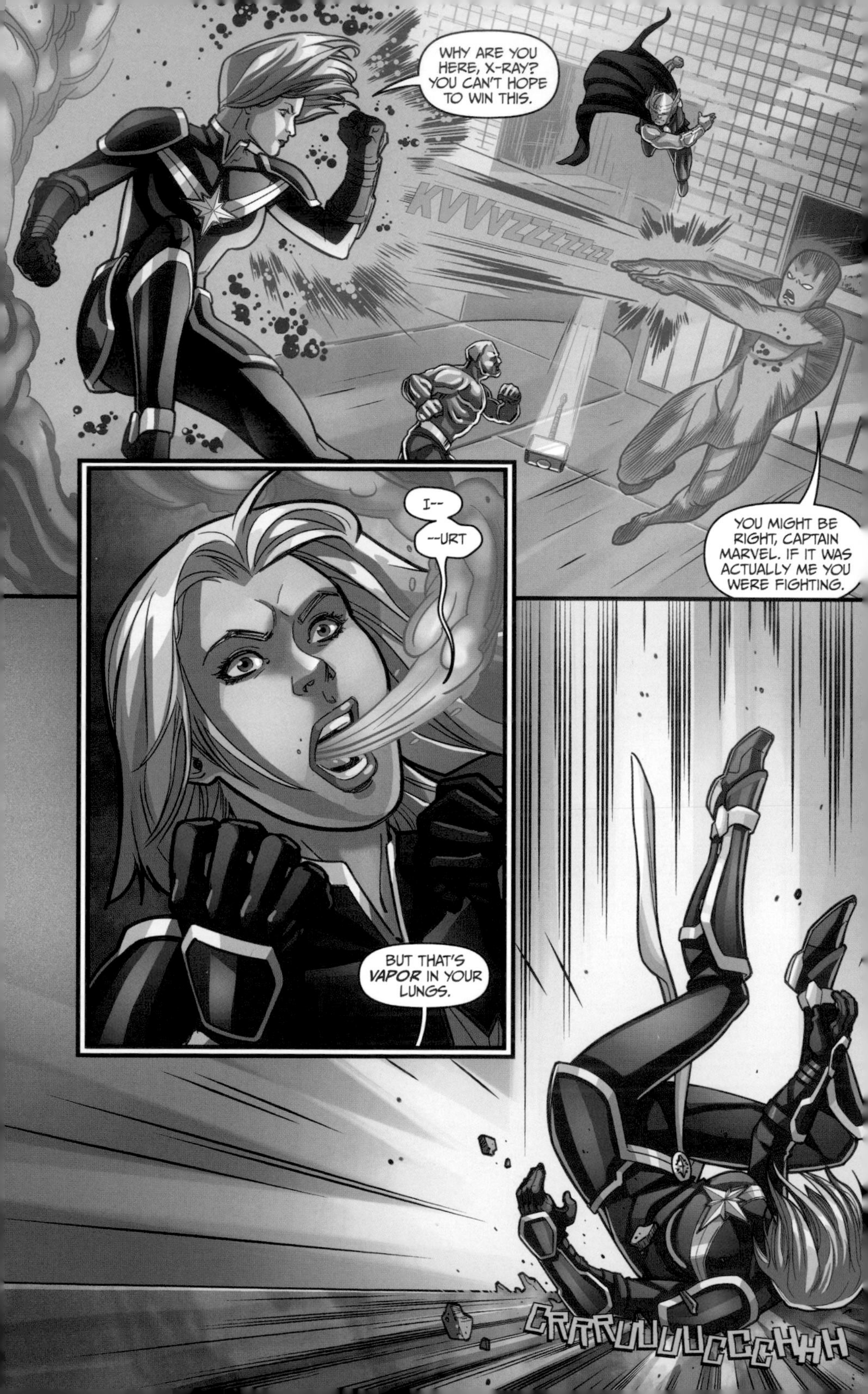
WHY ARE YOU HERE, X-RAY? YOU CAN'T HOPE TO WIN THIS.
KVVVZZZZZZZ
YOU MIGHT BE RIGHT, CAPTAIN MARVEL. IF IT WAS ACTUALLY ME YOU WERE FIGHTING.
I--
--URT
BUT THAT'S *VAPOR* IN YOUR LUNGS.
CRRRUUUUCCCCHHH

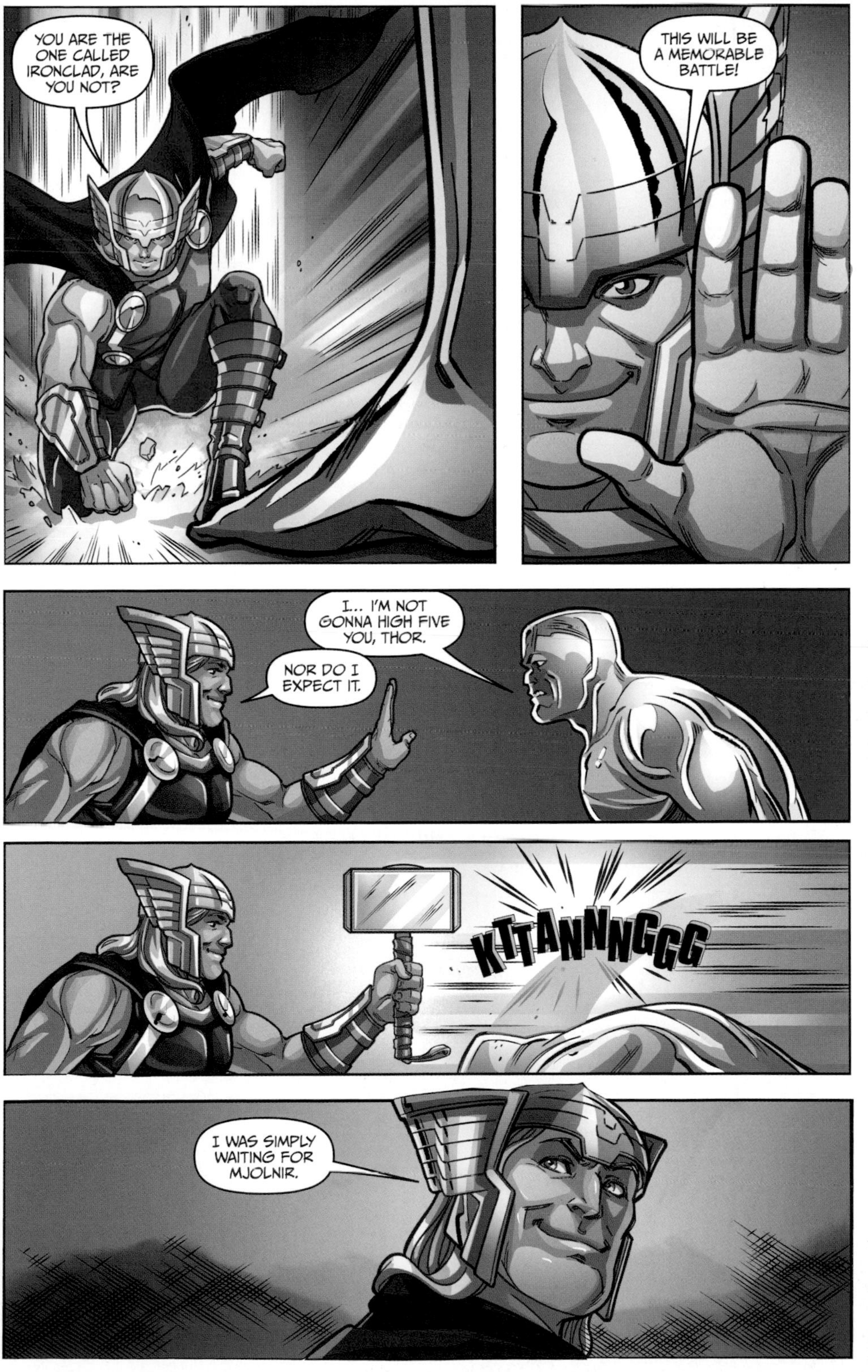
YOU ARE THE ONE CALLED IRONCLAD, ARE YOU NOT?
THIS WILL BE A MEMORABLE BATTLE!
I... I'M NOT GONNA HIGH FIVE YOU, THOR.
NOR DO I EXPECT IT.
KTTANNNGGG
I WAS SIMPLY WAITING FOR MJOLNIR.

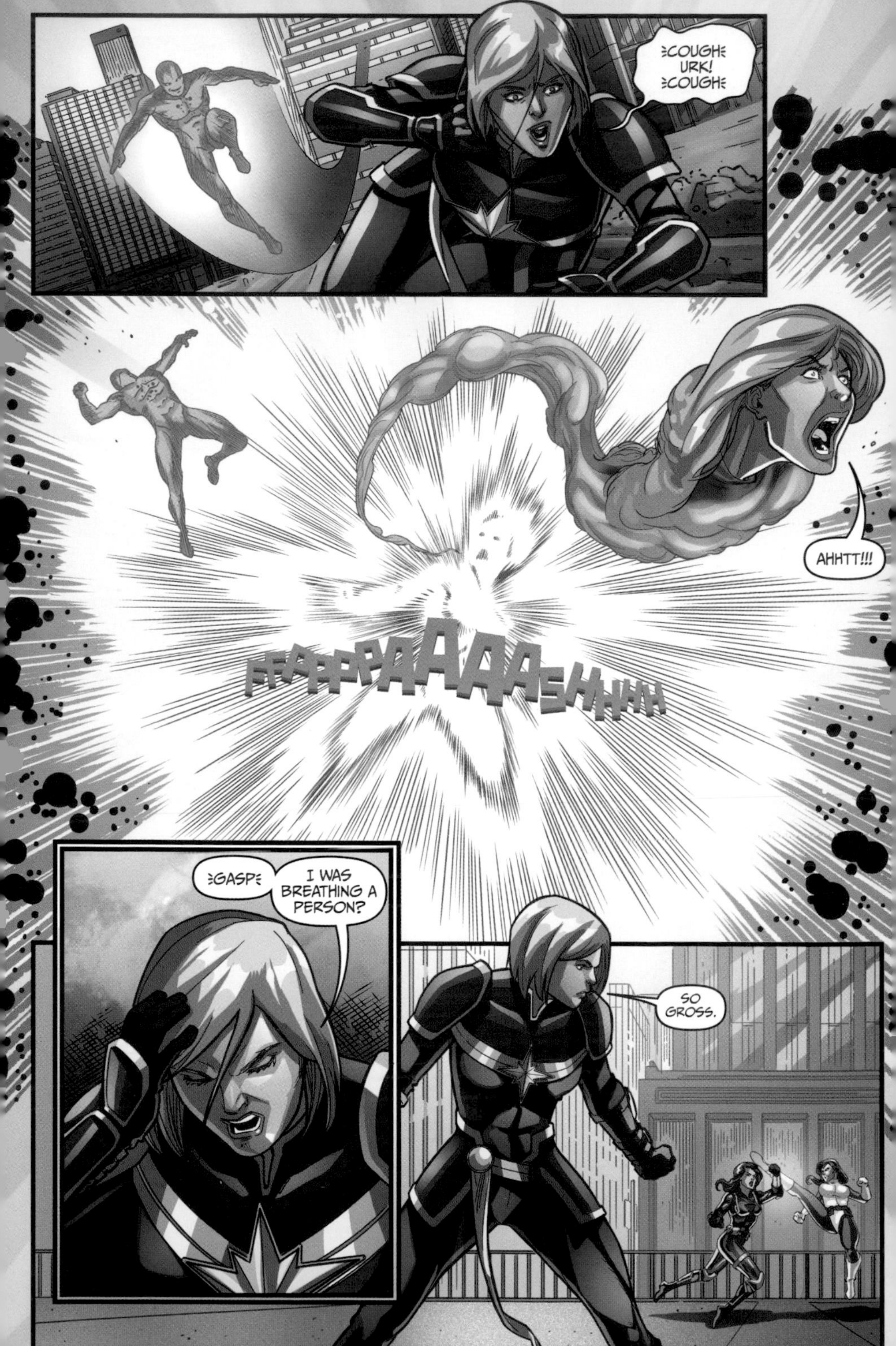

COUGH URK! COUGH
AHHTT!!!
FFFPPPPAAAAASHHHH
GASP
I WAS BREATHING A PERSON?
SO GROSS.

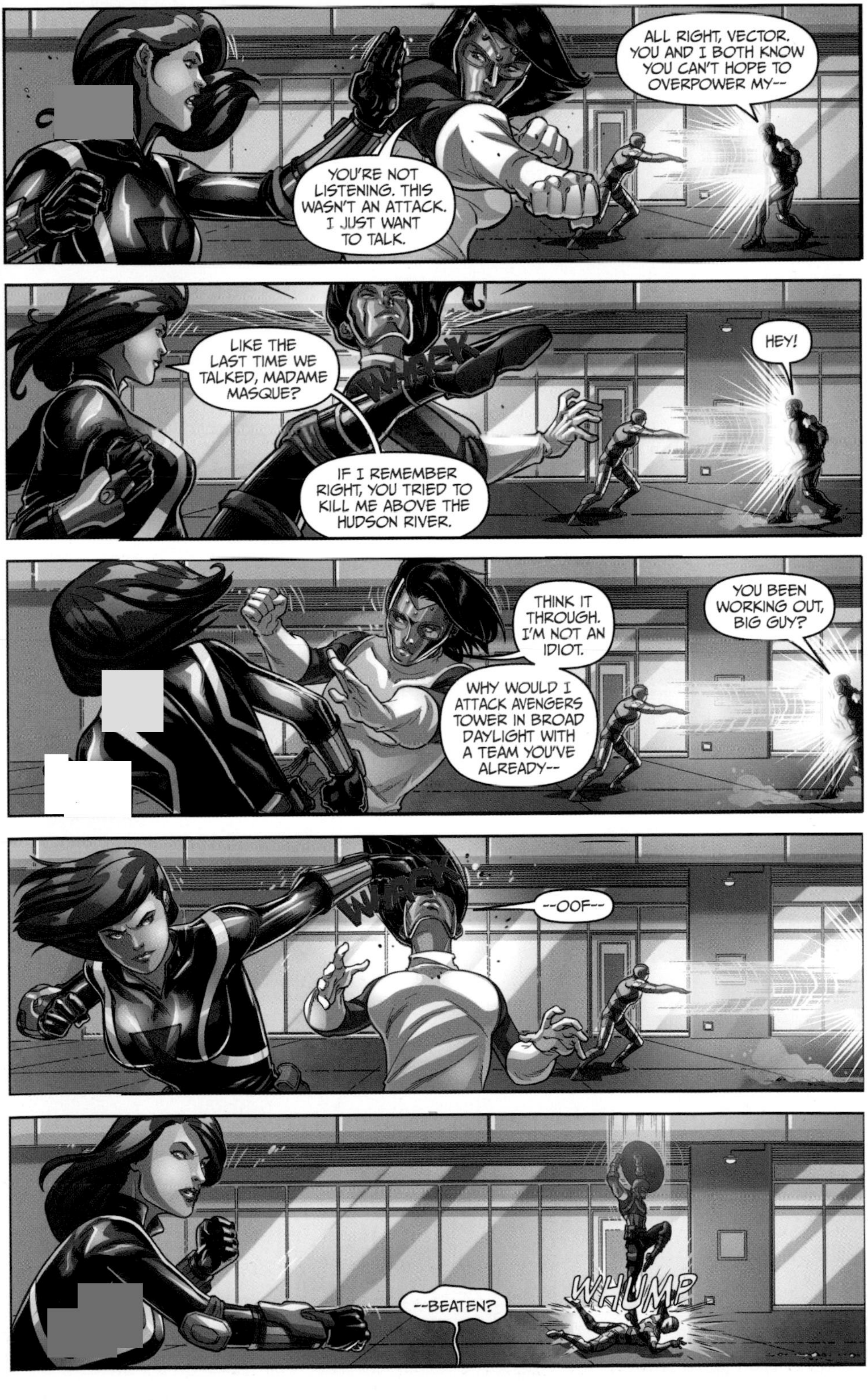
ALL RIGHT, VECTOR. YOU AND I BOTH KNOW YOU CAN'T HOPE TO OVERPOWER MY--
YOU'RE NOT LISTENING. THIS WASN'T AN ATTACK. I JUST WANT TO TALK.
WHACK
LIKE THE LAST TIME WE TALKED, MADAME MASQUE?
IF I REMEMBER RIGHT, YOU TRIED TO KILL ME ABOVE THE HUDSON RIVER.
HEY!
THINK IT THROUGH. I'M NOT AN IDIOT.
WHY WOULD I ATTACK AVENGERS TOWER IN BROAD DAYLIGHT WITH A TEAM YOU'VE ALREADY--
YOU BEEN WORKING OUT, BIG GUY?
WHACK
--OOF--
--BEATEN?
WHUMP

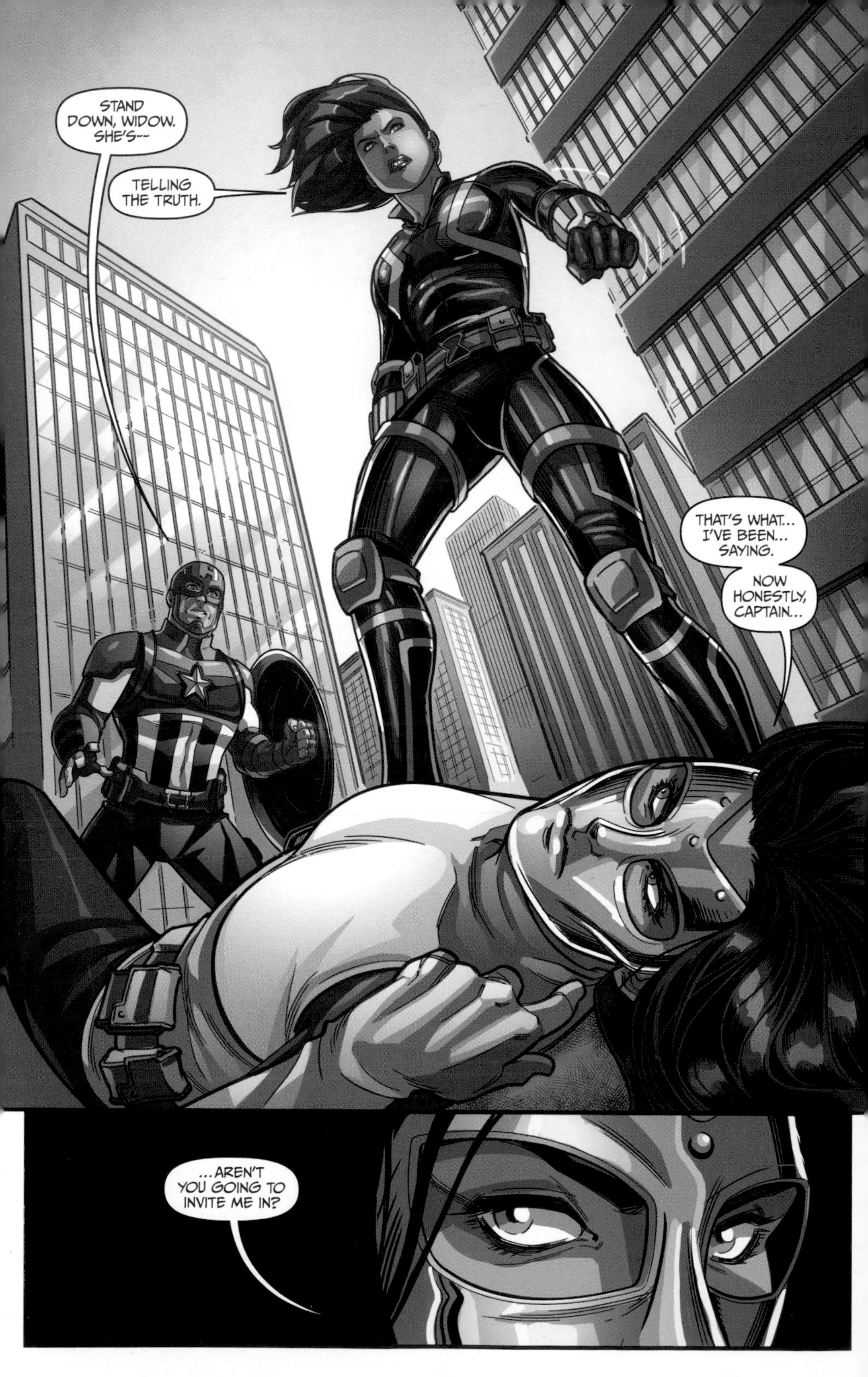
STAND DOWN, WIDOW. SHE'S--
TELLING THE TRUTH.
THAT'S WHAT... I'VE BEEN... SAYING.
NOW HONESTLY, CAPTAIN...
...AREN'T YOU GOING TO INVITE ME IN?

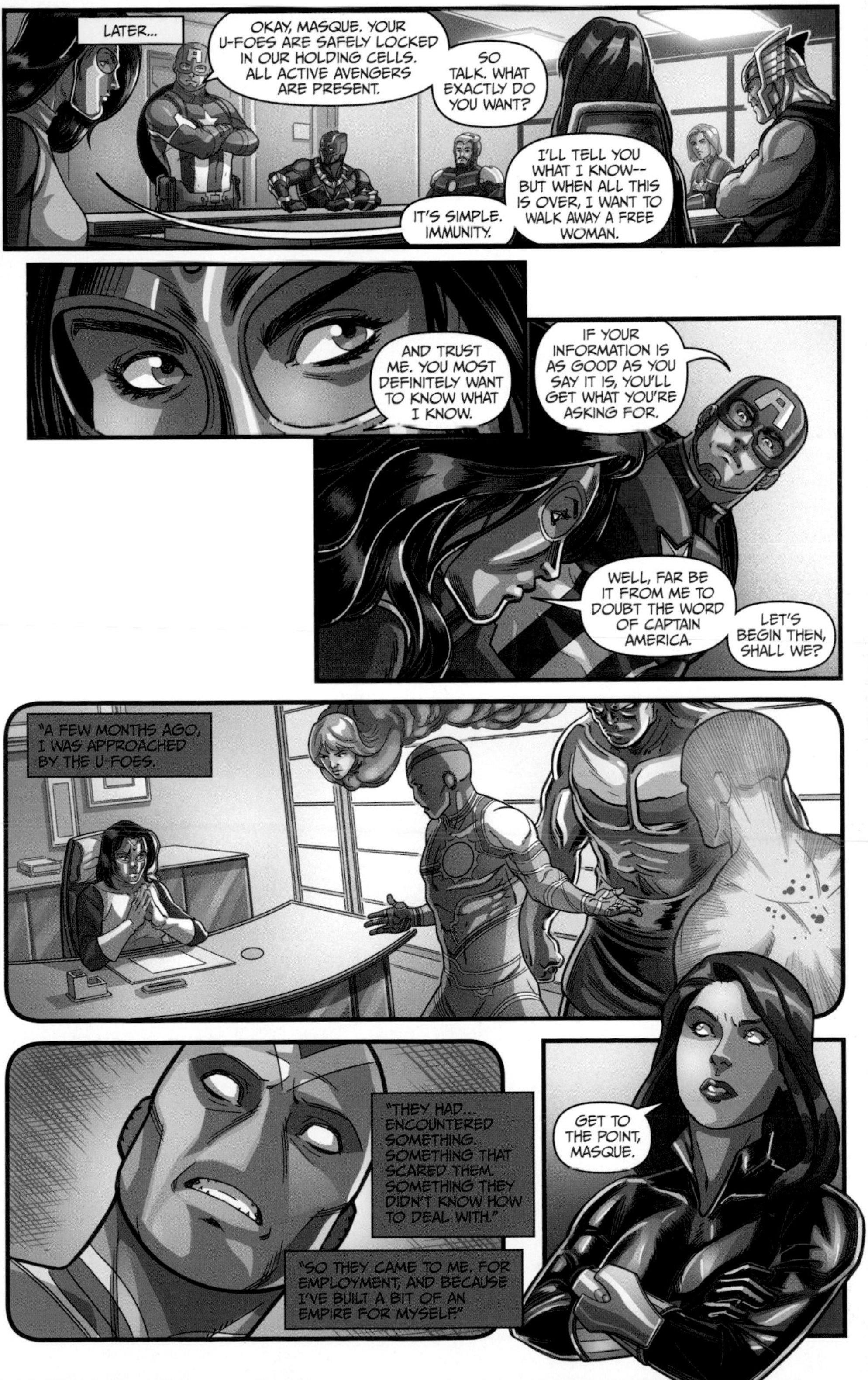
LATER...
OKAY, MASQUE. YOUR U-FOES ARE SAFELY LOCKED IN OUR HOLDING CELLS. ALL ACTIVE AVENGERS ARE PRESENT.
SO TALK. WHAT EXACTLY DO YOU WANT?
IT'S SIMPLE. IMMUNITY.
I'LL TELL YOU WHAT I KNOW-- BUT WHEN ALL THIS IS OVER, I WANT TO WALK AWAY A FREE WOMAN.
AND TRUST ME. YOU MOST DEFINITELY WANT TO KNOW WHAT I KNOW.
IF YOUR INFORMATION IS AS GOOD AS YOU SAY IT IS, YOU'LL GET WHAT YOU'RE ASKING FOR.
WELL, FAR BE IT FROM ME TO DOUBT THE WORD OF CAPTAIN AMERICA.
LET'S BEGIN THEN, SHALL WE?
"A FEW MONTHS AGO, I WAS APPROACHED BY THE U-FOES.
"THEY HAD... ENCOUNTERED SOMETHING. SOMETHING THAT SCARED THEM. SOMETHING THEY DIDN'T KNOW HOW TO DEAL WITH."
"SO THEY CAME TO ME. FOR EMPLOYMENT, AND BECAUSE I'VE BUILT A BIT OF AN EMPIRE FOR MYSELF."
GET TO THE POINT, MASQUE.

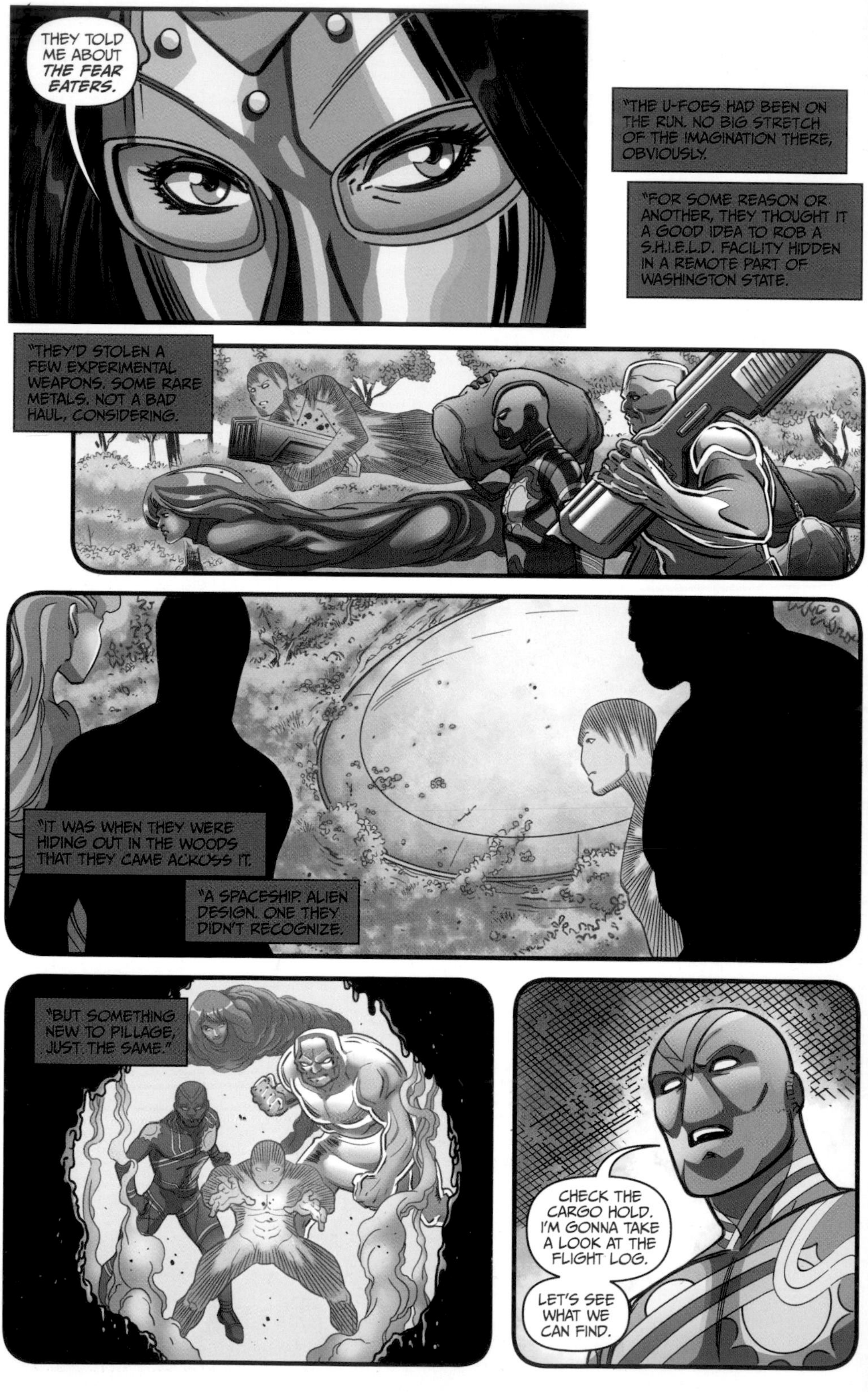
THEY TOLD ME ABOUT *THE FEAR EATERS.*
"THE U-FOES HAD BEEN ON THE RUN. NO BIG STRETCH OF THE IMAGINATION THERE, OBVIOUSLY.
"FOR SOME REASON OR ANOTHER, THEY THOUGHT IT A GOOD IDEA TO ROB A S.H.I.E.L.D. FACILITY HIDDEN IN A REMOTE PART OF WASHINGTON STATE.
"THEY'D STOLEN A FEW EXPERIMENTAL WEAPONS. SOME RARE METALS. NOT A BAD HAUL, CONSIDERING.
"IT WAS WHEN THEY WERE HIDING OUT IN THE WOODS THAT THEY CAME ACROSS IT.
"A SPACESHIP. ALIEN DESIGN. ONE THEY DIDN'T RECOGNIZE.
"BUT SOMETHING NEW TO PILLAGE, JUST THE SAME."
CHECK THE CARGO HOLD. I'M GONNA TAKE A LOOK AT THE FLIGHT LOG.
LET'S SEE WHAT WE CAN FIND.

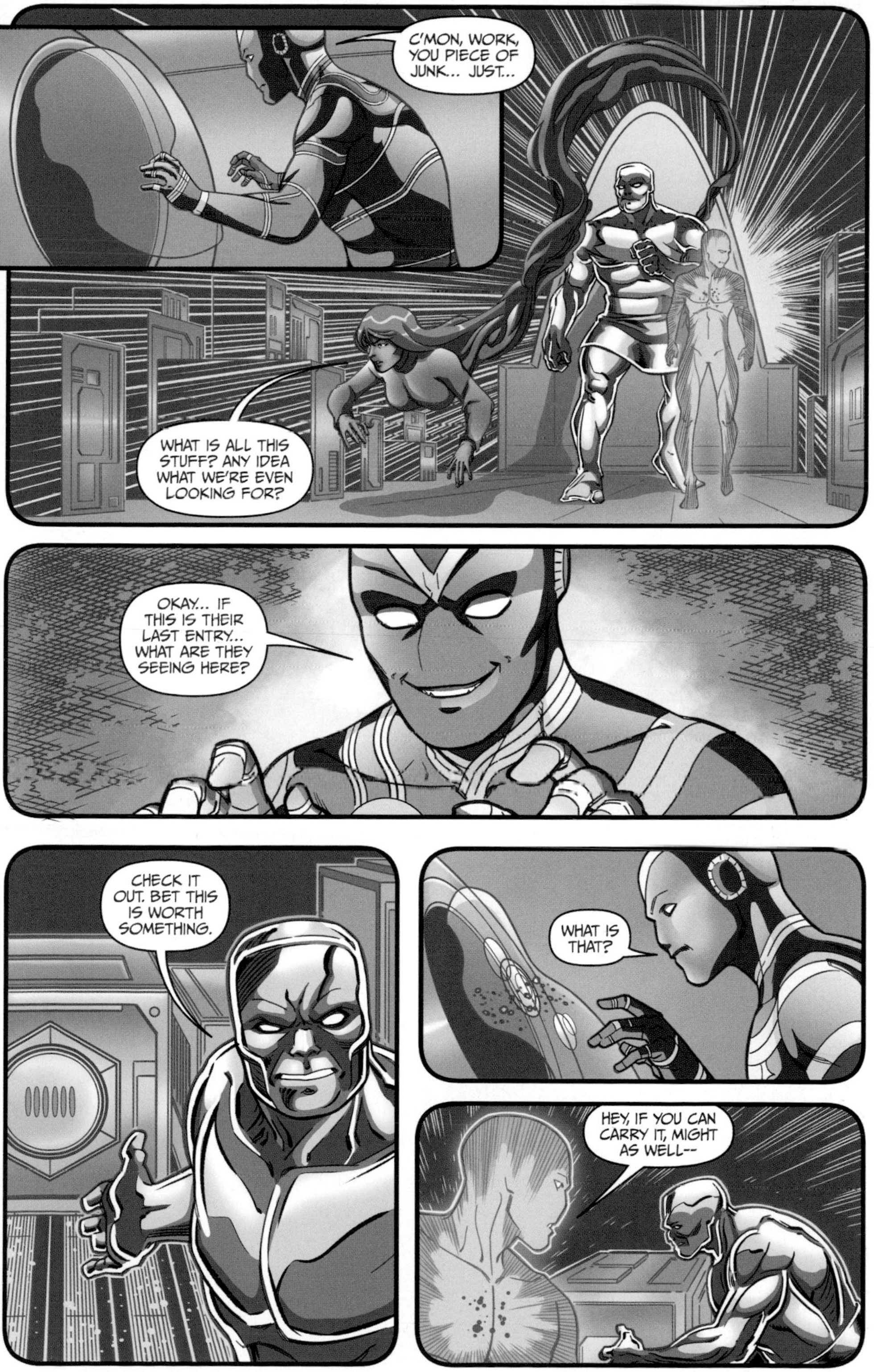
C'MON, WORK, YOU PIECE OF JUNK... JUST...
WHAT IS ALL THIS STUFF? ANY IDEA WHAT WE'RE EVEN LOOKING FOR?
OKAY... IF THIS IS THEIR LAST ENTRY... WHAT ARE THEY SEEING HERE?
CHECK IT OUT. BET THIS IS WORTH SOMETHING.
WHAT IS THAT?
HEY, IF YOU CAN CARRY IT, MIGHT AS WELL--

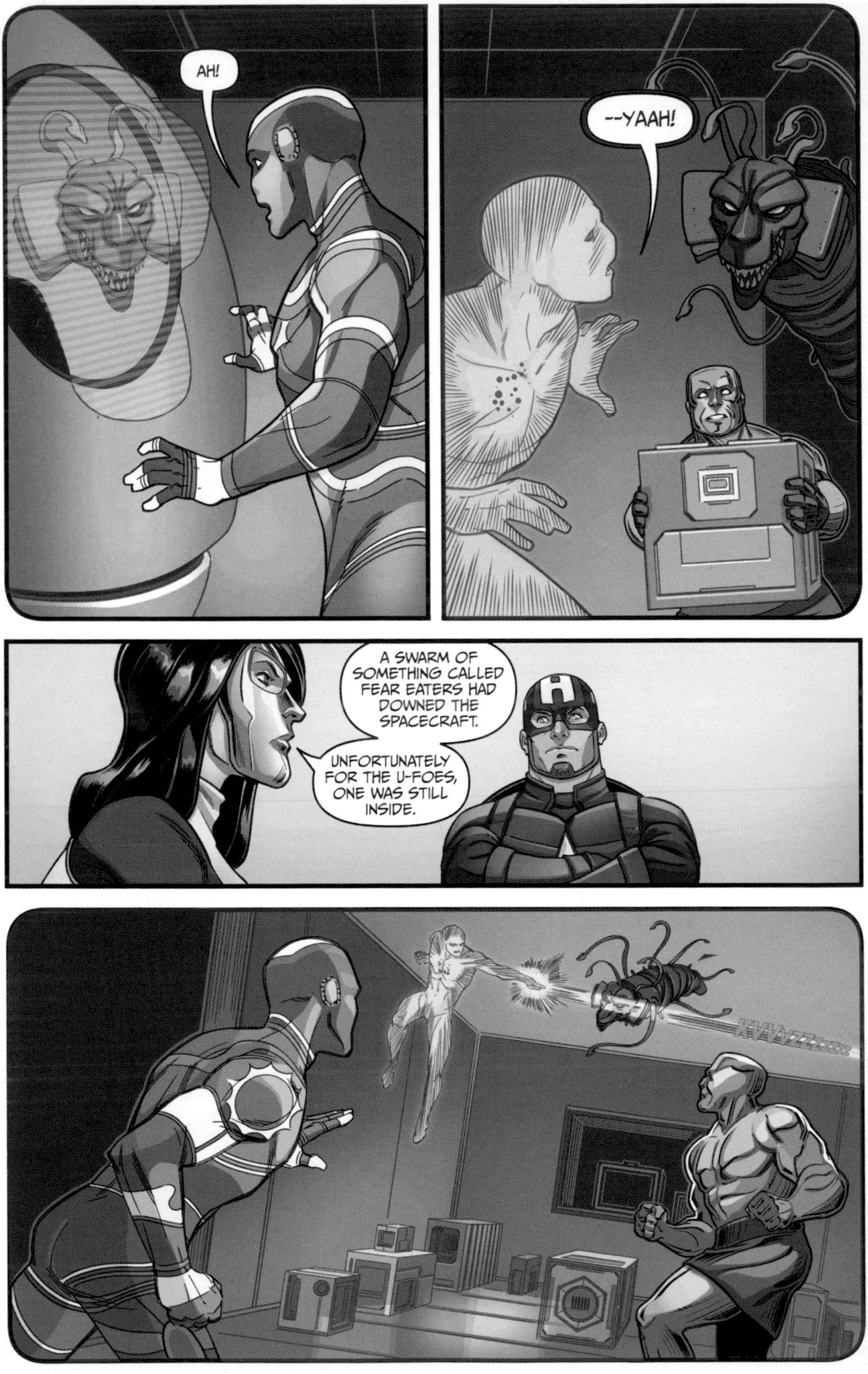
AH!
--YAAH!
A SWARM OF SOMETHING CALLED FEAR EATERS HAD DOWNED THE SPACECRAFT.
UNFORTUNATELY FOR THE U-FOES, ONE WAS STILL INSIDE.
KVVVZZZzzz

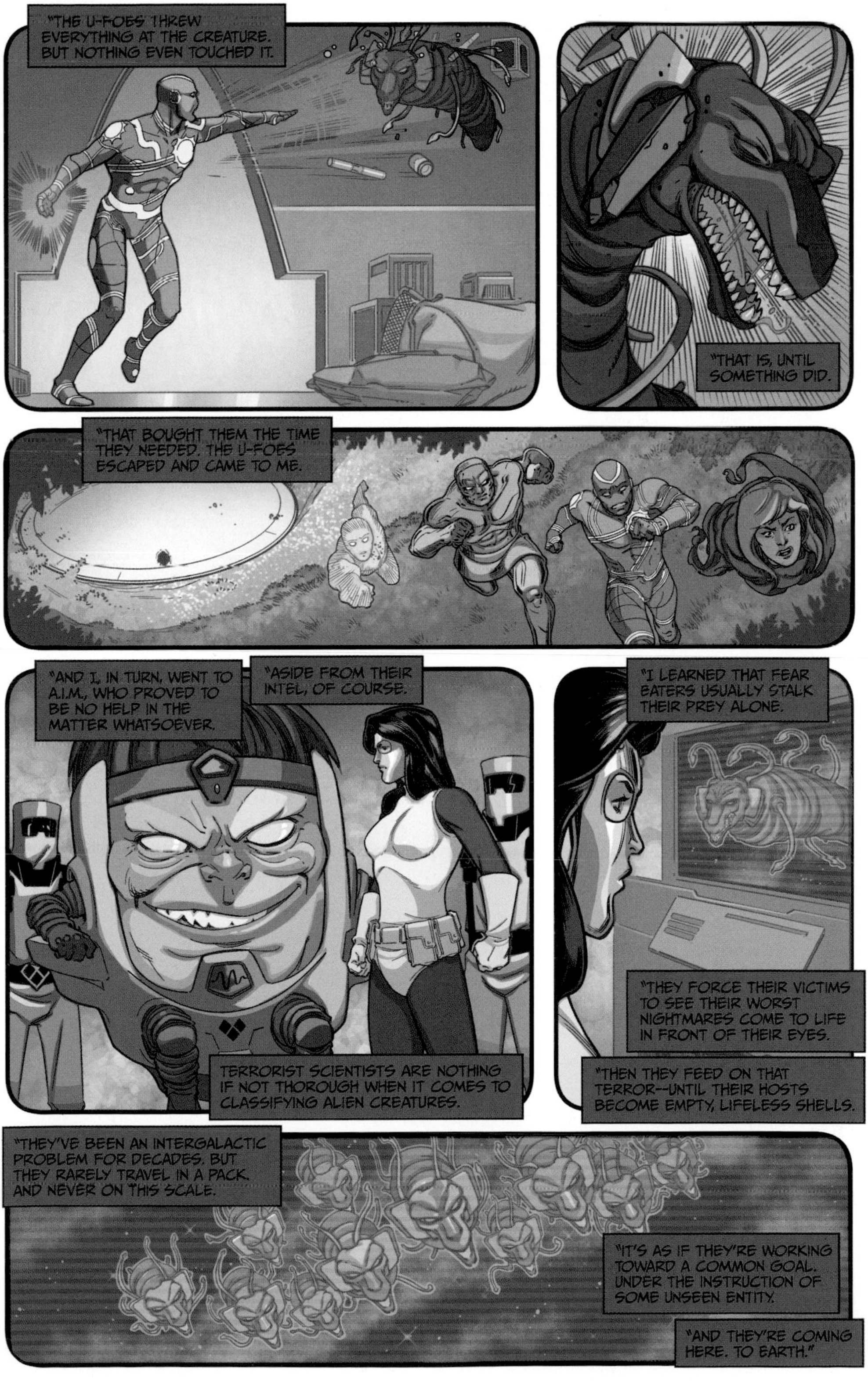
"THE U-FOES THREW EVERYTHING AT THE CREATURE. BUT NOTHING EVEN TOUCHED IT.
"THAT IS, UNTIL SOMETHING DID.
"THAT BOUGHT THEM THE TIME THEY NEEDED. THE U-FOES ESCAPED AND CAME TO ME.
"AND I, IN TURN, WENT TO A.I.M., WHO PROVED TO BE NO HELP IN THE MATTER WHATSOEVER.
"ASIDE FROM THEIR INTEL, OF COURSE.
TERRORIST SCIENTISTS ARE NOTHING IF NOT THOROUGH WHEN IT COMES TO CLASSIFYING ALIEN CREATURES.
"I LEARNED THAT FEAR EATERS USUALLY STALK THEIR PREY ALONE.
"THEY FORCE THEIR VICTIMS TO SEE THEIR WORST NIGHTMARES COME TO LIFE IN FRONT OF THEIR EYES.
"THEN THEY FEED ON THAT TERROR--UNTIL THEIR HOSTS BECOME EMPTY, LIFELESS SHELLS.
"THEY'VE BEEN AN INTERGALACTIC PROBLEM FOR DECADES. BUT THEY RARELY TRAVEL IN A PACK. AND NEVER ON THIS SCALE.
"IT'S AS IF THEY'RE WORKING TOWARD A COMMON GOAL. UNDER THE INSTRUCTION OF SOME UNSEEN ENTITY.
"AND THEY'RE COMING HERE. TO EARTH."

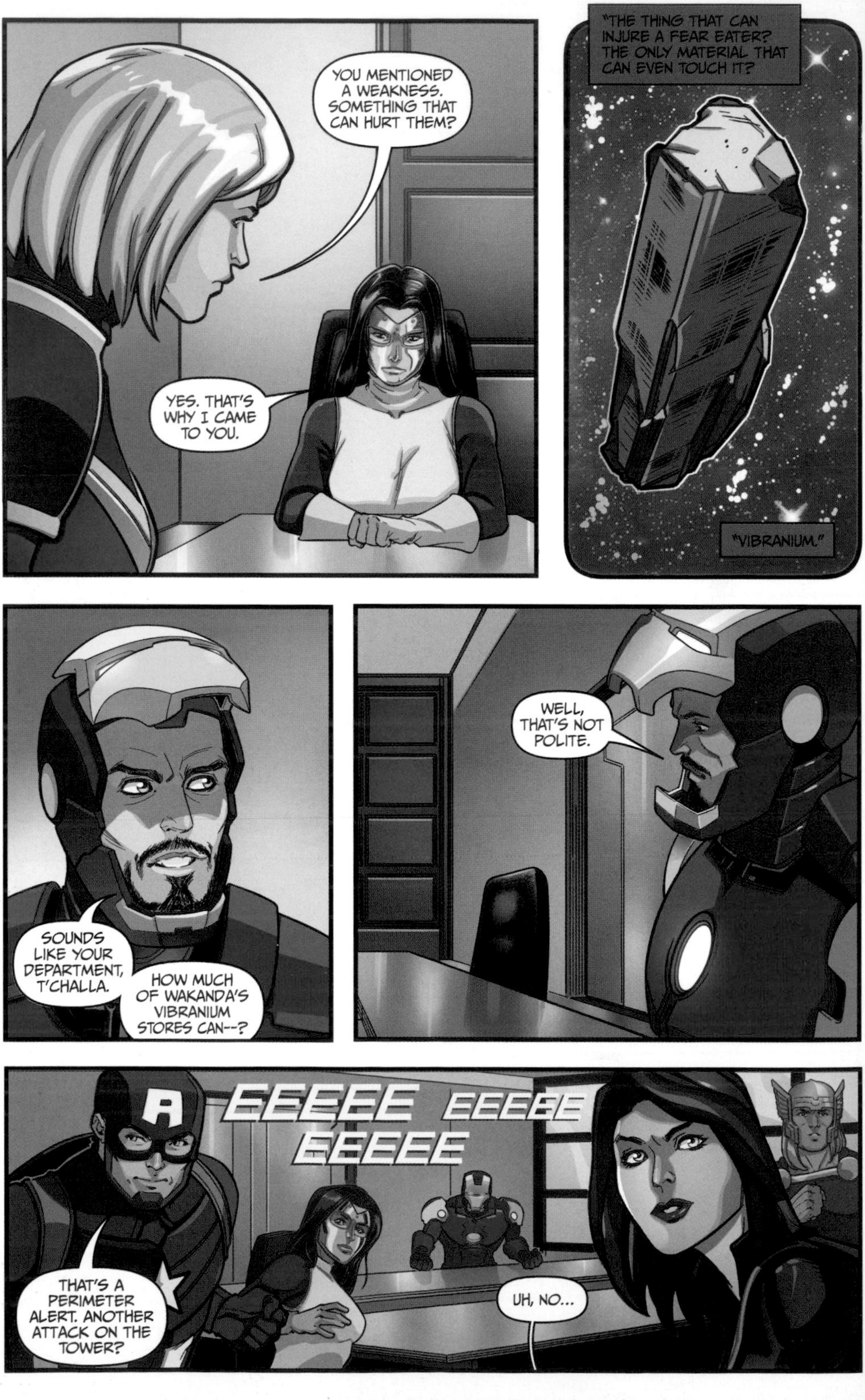
YOU MENTIONED A WEAKNESS. SOMETHING THAT CAN HURT THEM?
YES. THAT'S WHY I CAME TO YOU.
"THE THING THAT CAN INJURE A FEAR EATER? THE ONLY MATERIAL THAT CAN EVEN TOUCH IT?
"VIBRANIUM."
SOUNDS LIKE YOUR DEPARTMENT, T'CHALLA.
HOW MUCH OF WAKANDA'S VIBRANIUM STORES CAN--?
WELL, THAT'S NOT POLITE.
EEEEE EEEEE EEEEE
THAT'S A PERIMETER ALERT. ANOTHER ATTACK ON THE TOWER?
UH, NO...

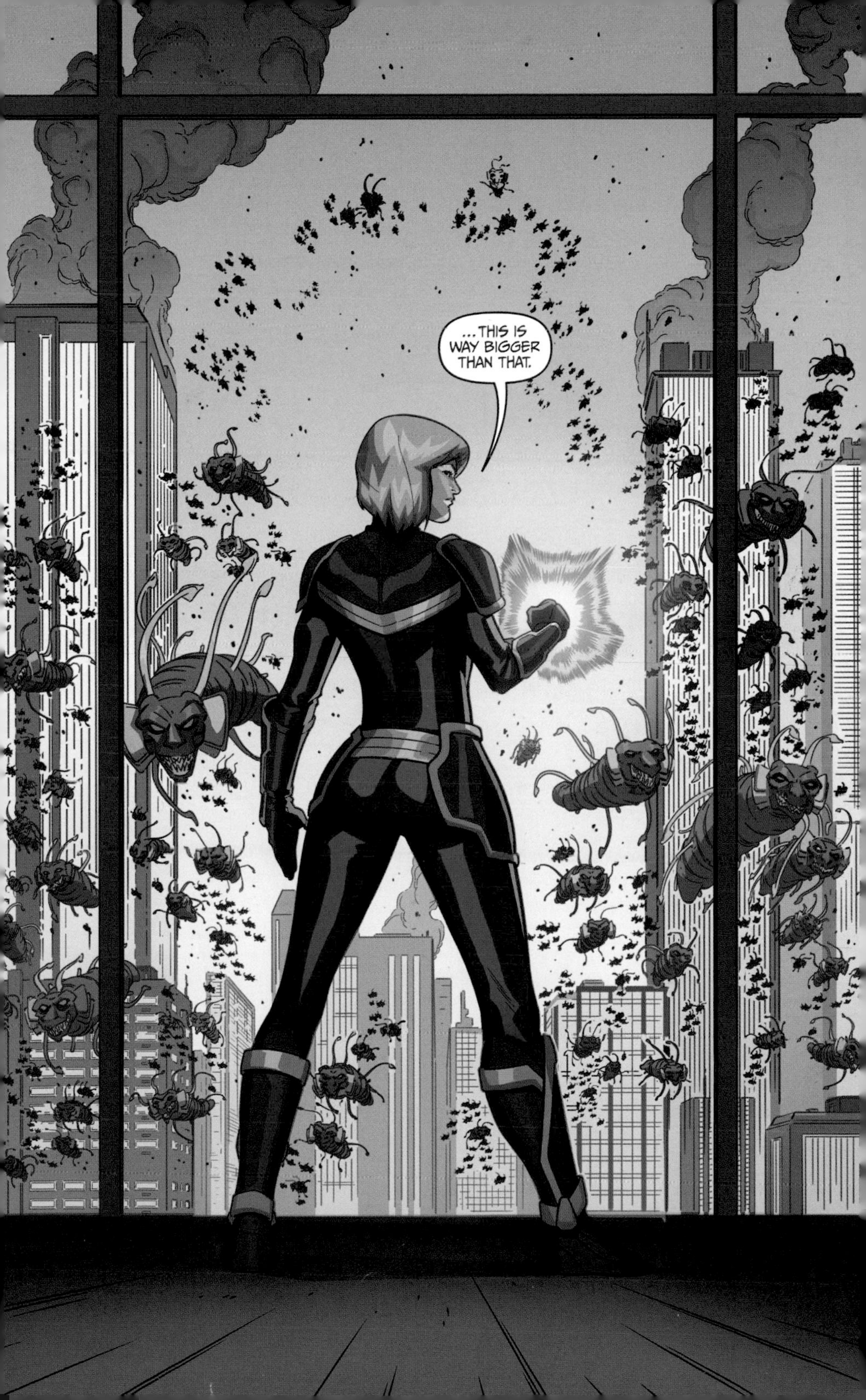
...THIS IS WAY BIGGER THAN THAT.

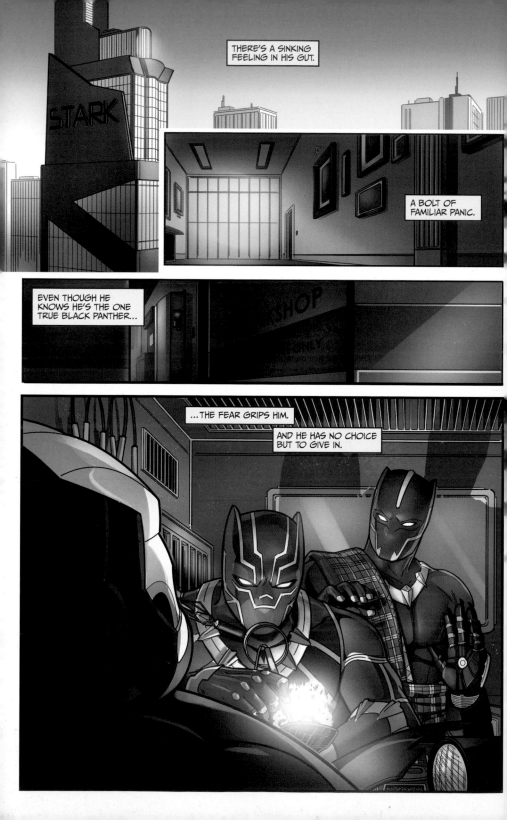

THERE'S A SINKING FEELING IN HIS GUT.

A BOLT OF FAMILIAR PANIC.

EVEN THOUGH HE KNOWS HE'S THE ONE TRUE BLACK PANTHER...

...THE FEAR GRIPS HIM.

AND HE HAS NO CHOICE BUT TO GIVE IN.

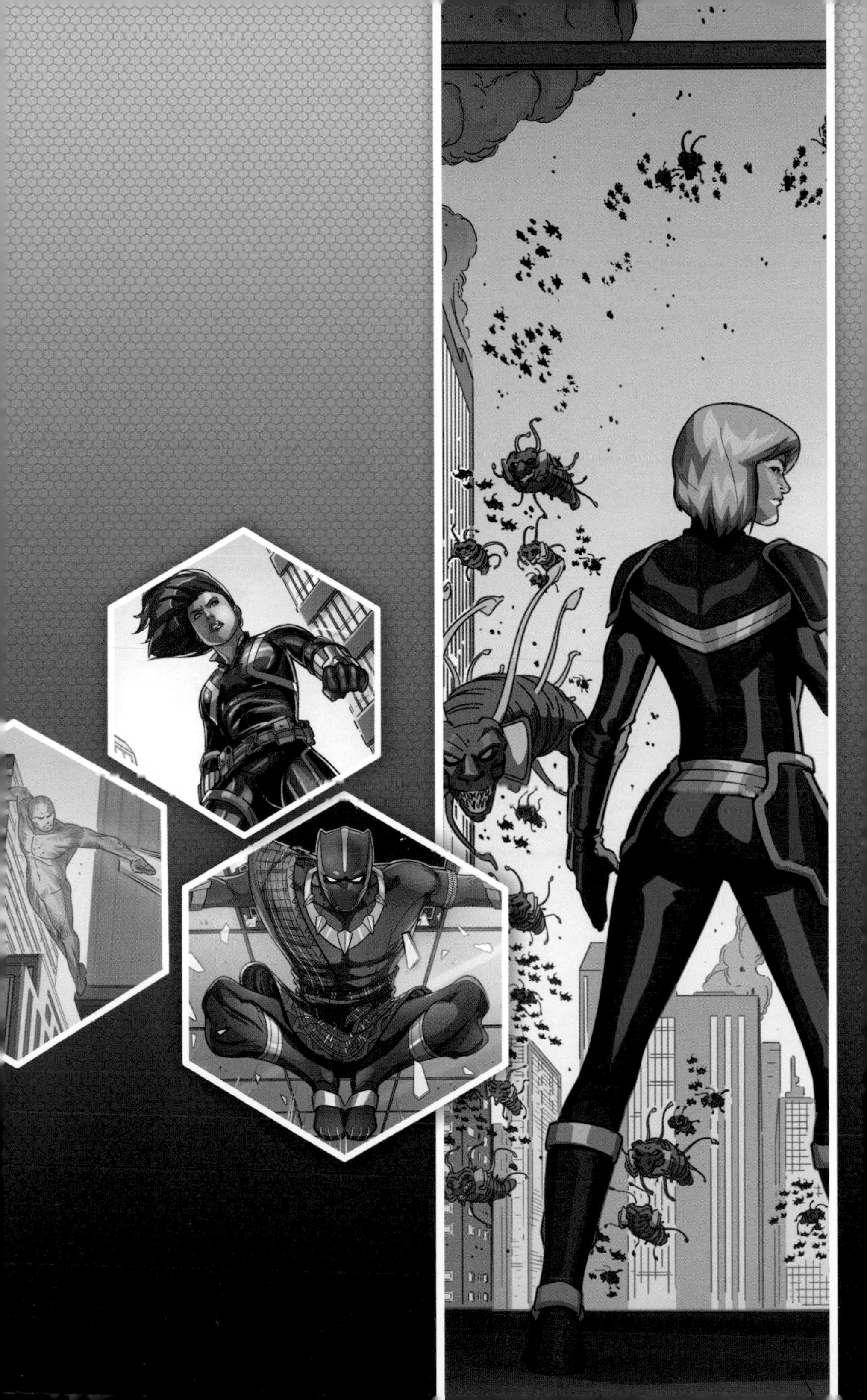

ART BY: JON SOMMARIVA
COLORS BY: PAC 23

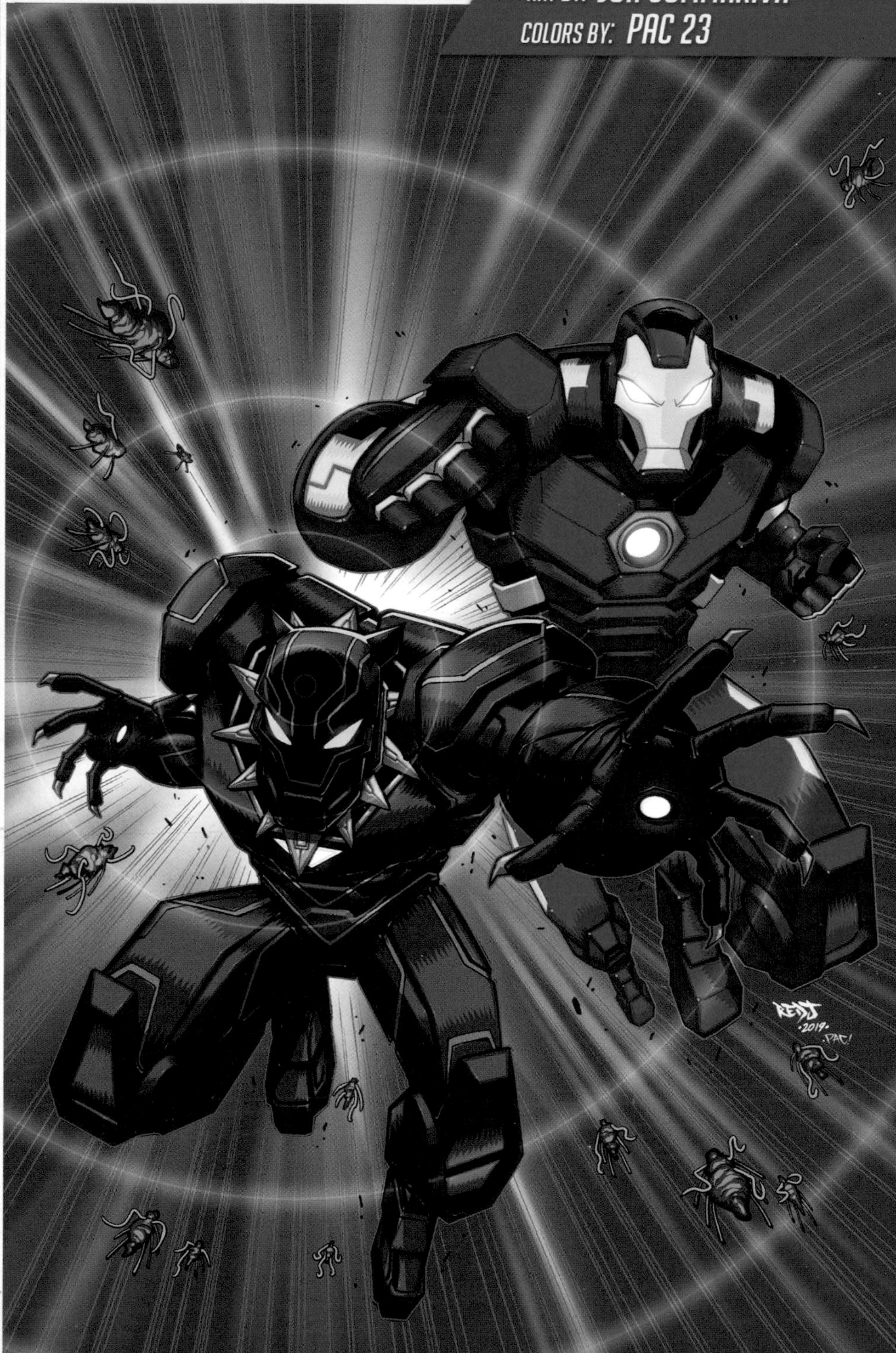

REDJ
2019
PAC!

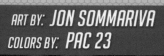

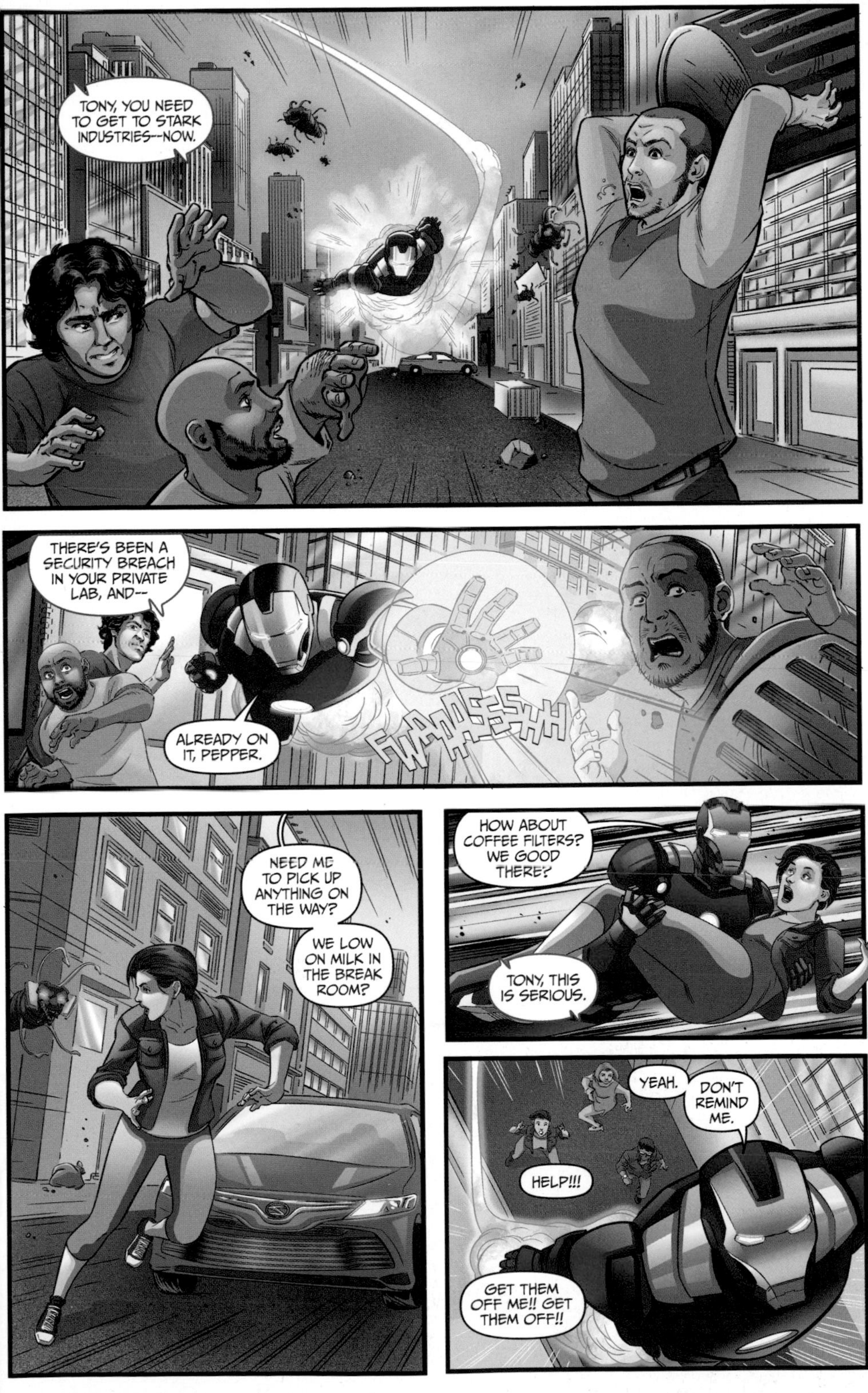
TONY, YOU NEED TO GET TO STARK INDUSTRIES--NOW.
THERE'S BEEN A SECURITY BREACH IN YOUR PRIVATE LAB, AND--
ALREADY ON IT, PEPPER.
FWOOOSHH
NEED ME TO PICK UP ANYTHING ON THE WAY?
WE LOW ON MILK IN THE BREAK ROOM?
HOW ABOUT COFFEE FILTERS? WE GOOD THERE?
TONY, THIS IS SERIOUS.
YEAH.
DON'T REMIND ME.
HELP!!!
GET THEM OFF ME!! GET THEM OFF!!

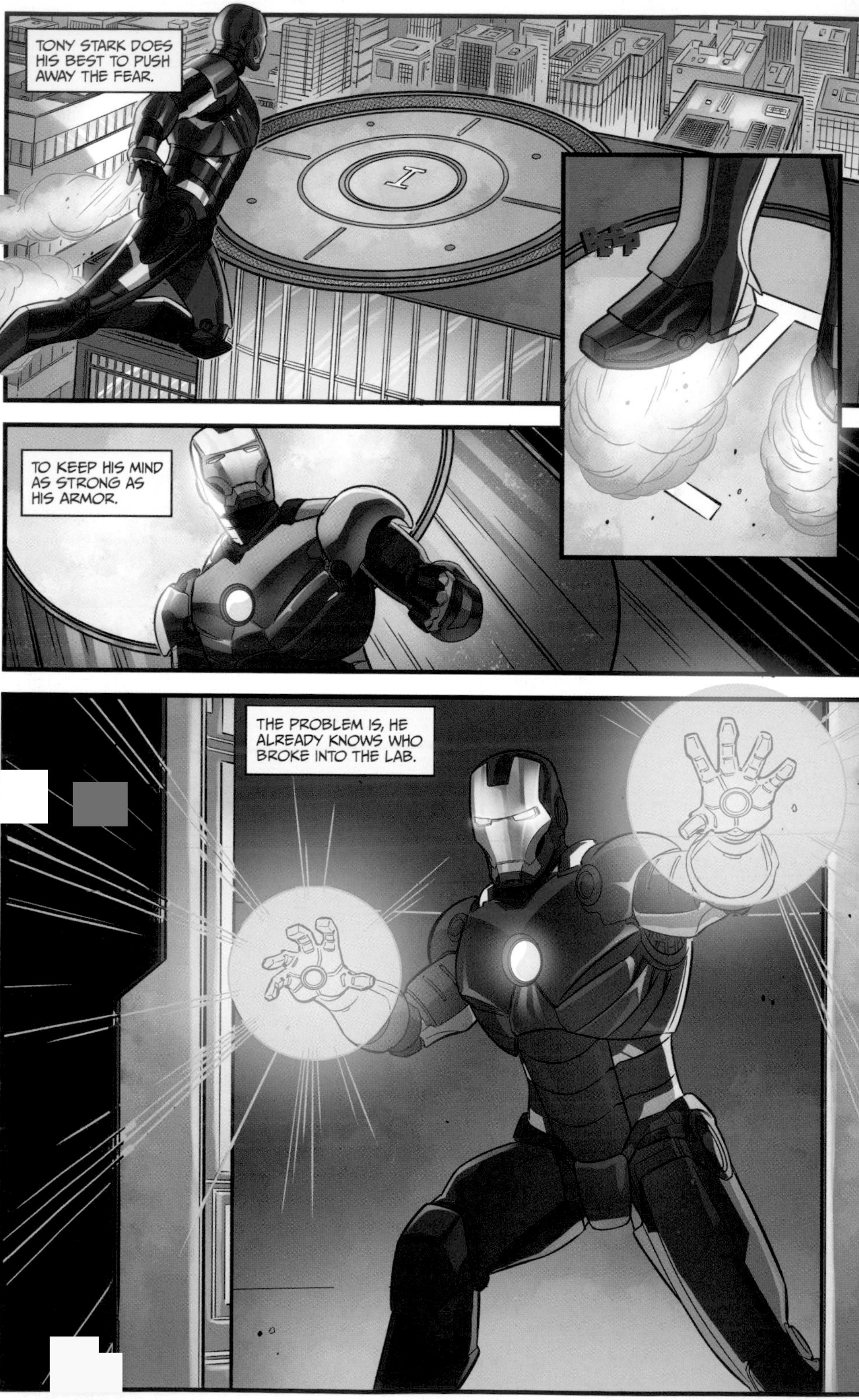
TONY STARK DOES HIS BEST TO PUSH AWAY THE FEAR.
TO KEEP HIS MIND AS STRONG AS HIS ARMOR.
THE PROBLEM IS, HE ALREADY KNOWS WHO BROKE INTO THE LAB.

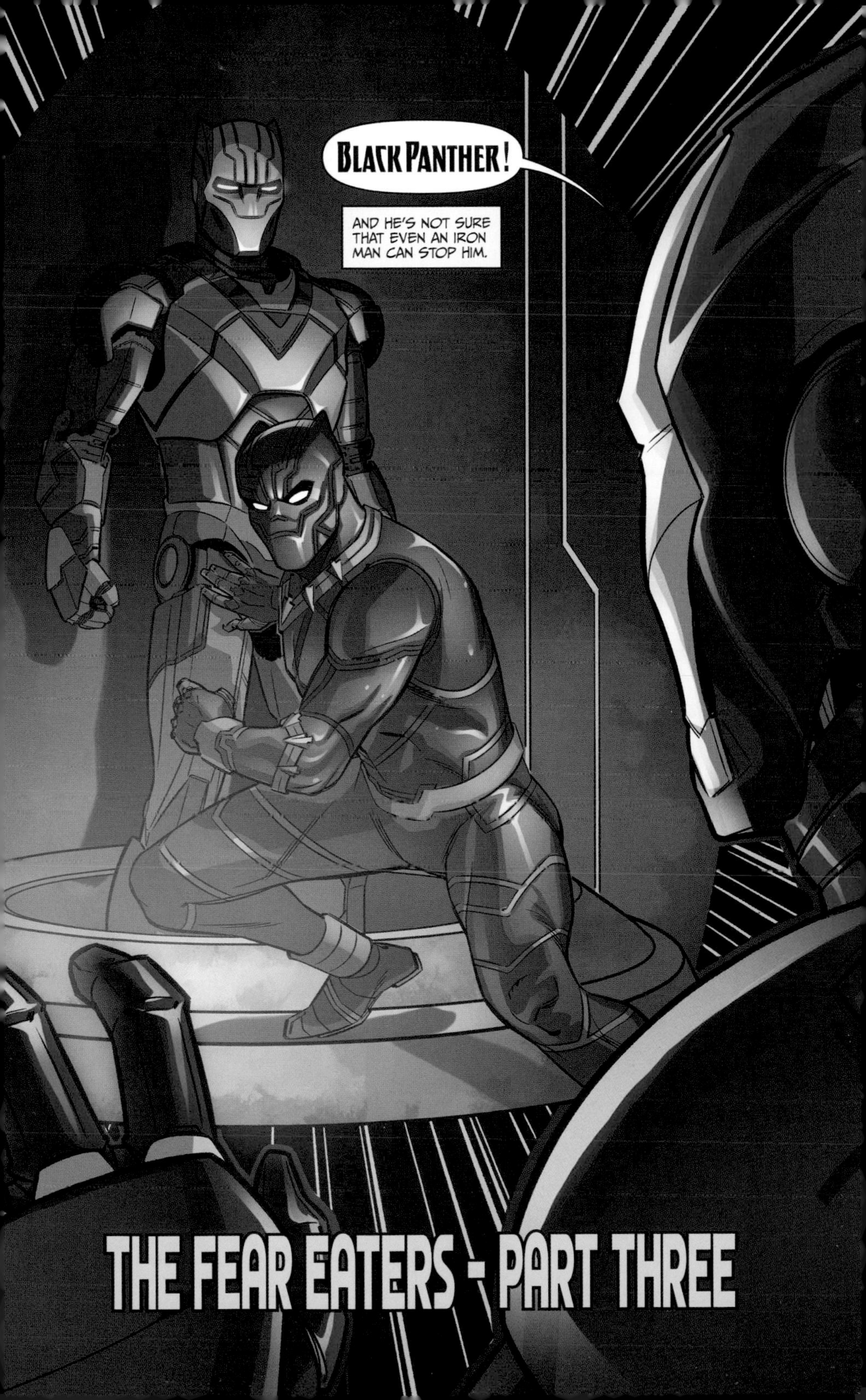
BLACK PANTHER!
AND HE'S NOT SURE THAT EVEN AN IRON MAN CAN STOP HIM.
THE FEAR EATERS - PART THREE

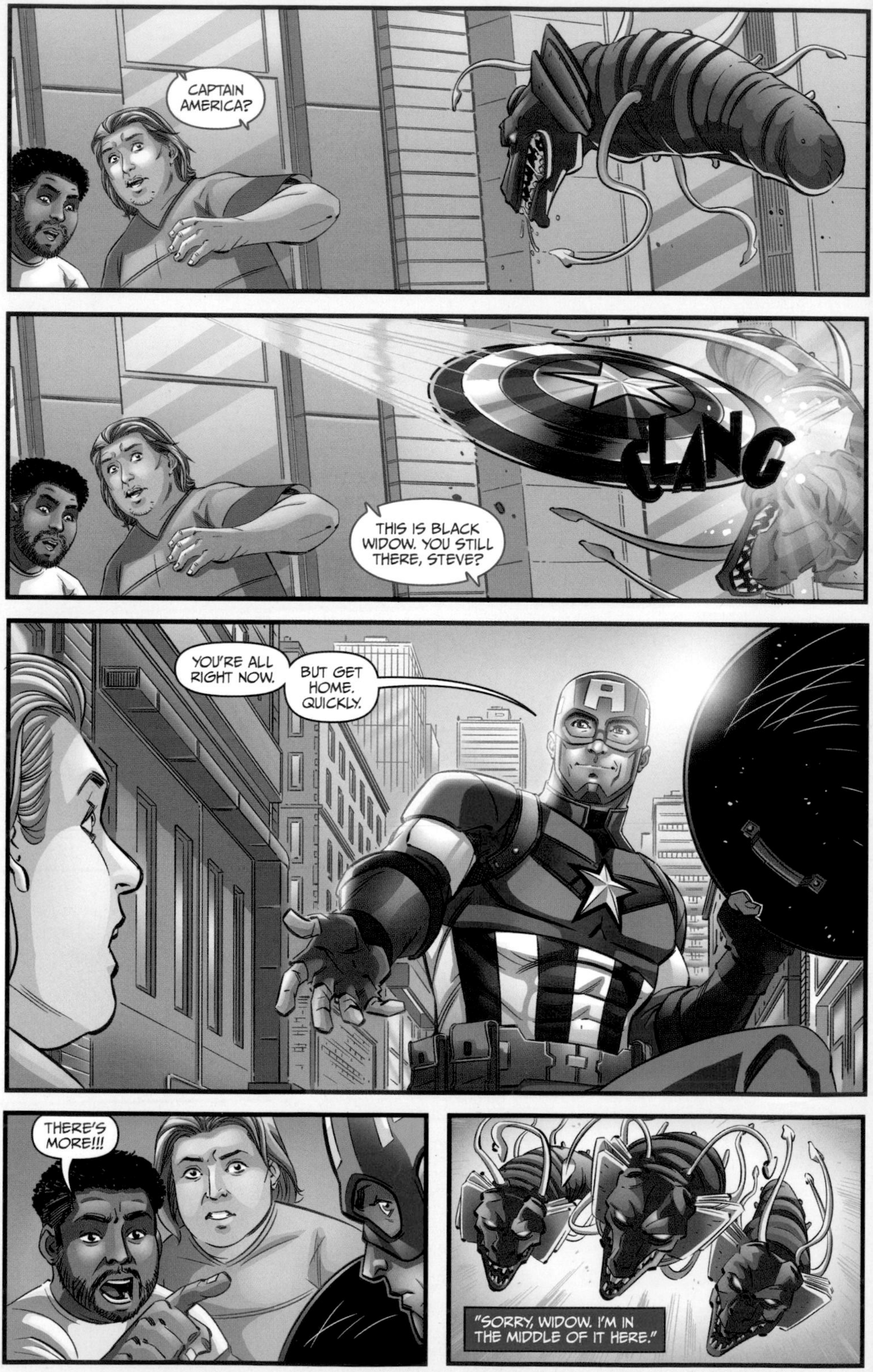
CAPTAIN AMERICA?
CLANG
THIS IS BLACK WIDOW. YOU STILL THERE, STEVE?
YOU'RE ALL RIGHT NOW.
BUT GET HOME. QUICKLY.
THERE'S MORE!!!
"SORRY, WIDOW. I'M IN THE MIDDLE OF IT HERE."

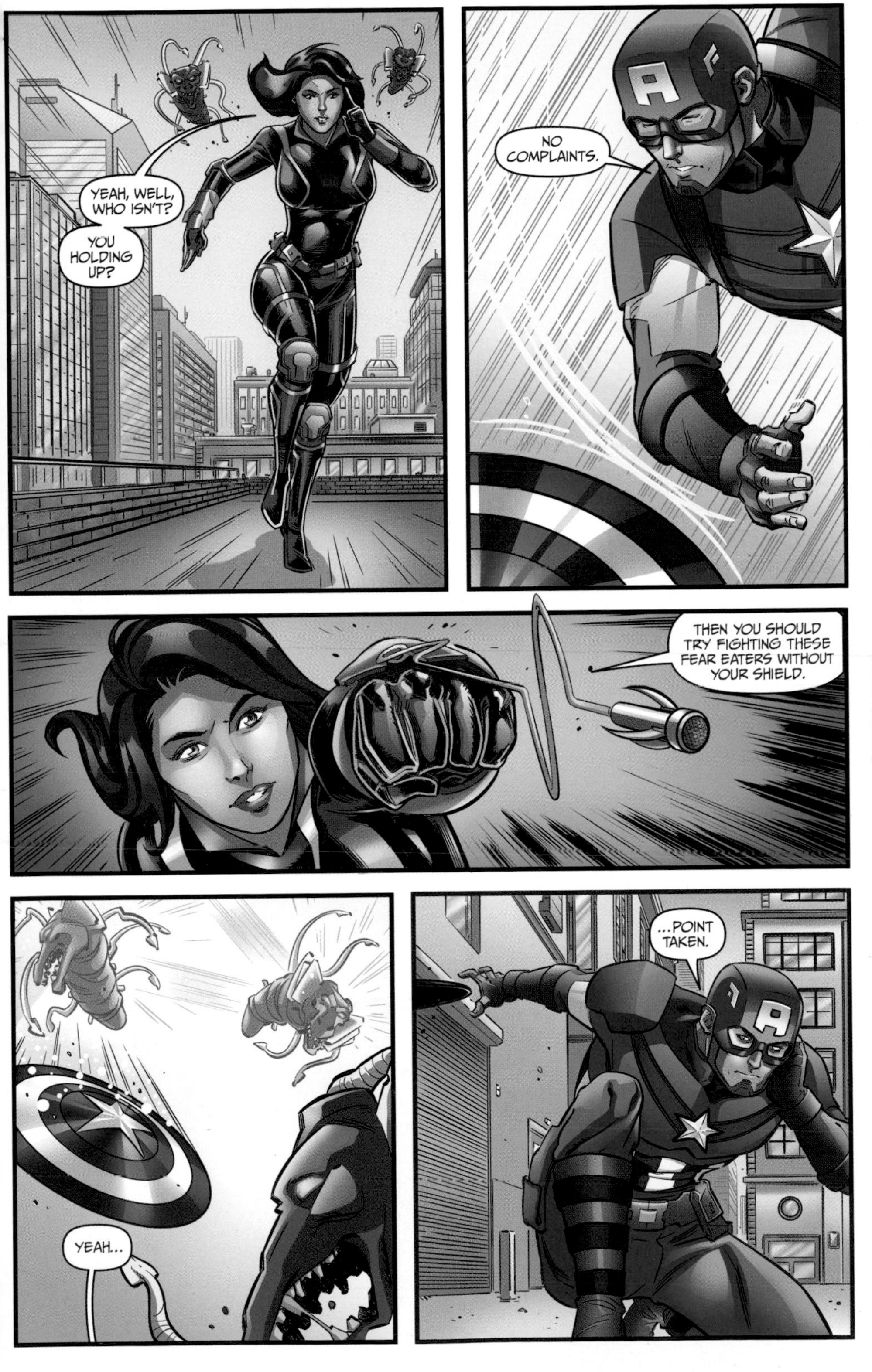
YEAH, WELL, WHO ISN'T?
YOU HOLDING UP?
NO COMPLAINTS.
THEN YOU SHOULD TRY FIGHTING THESE FEAR EATERS WITHOUT YOUR SHIELD.
YEAH...
...POINT TAKEN.

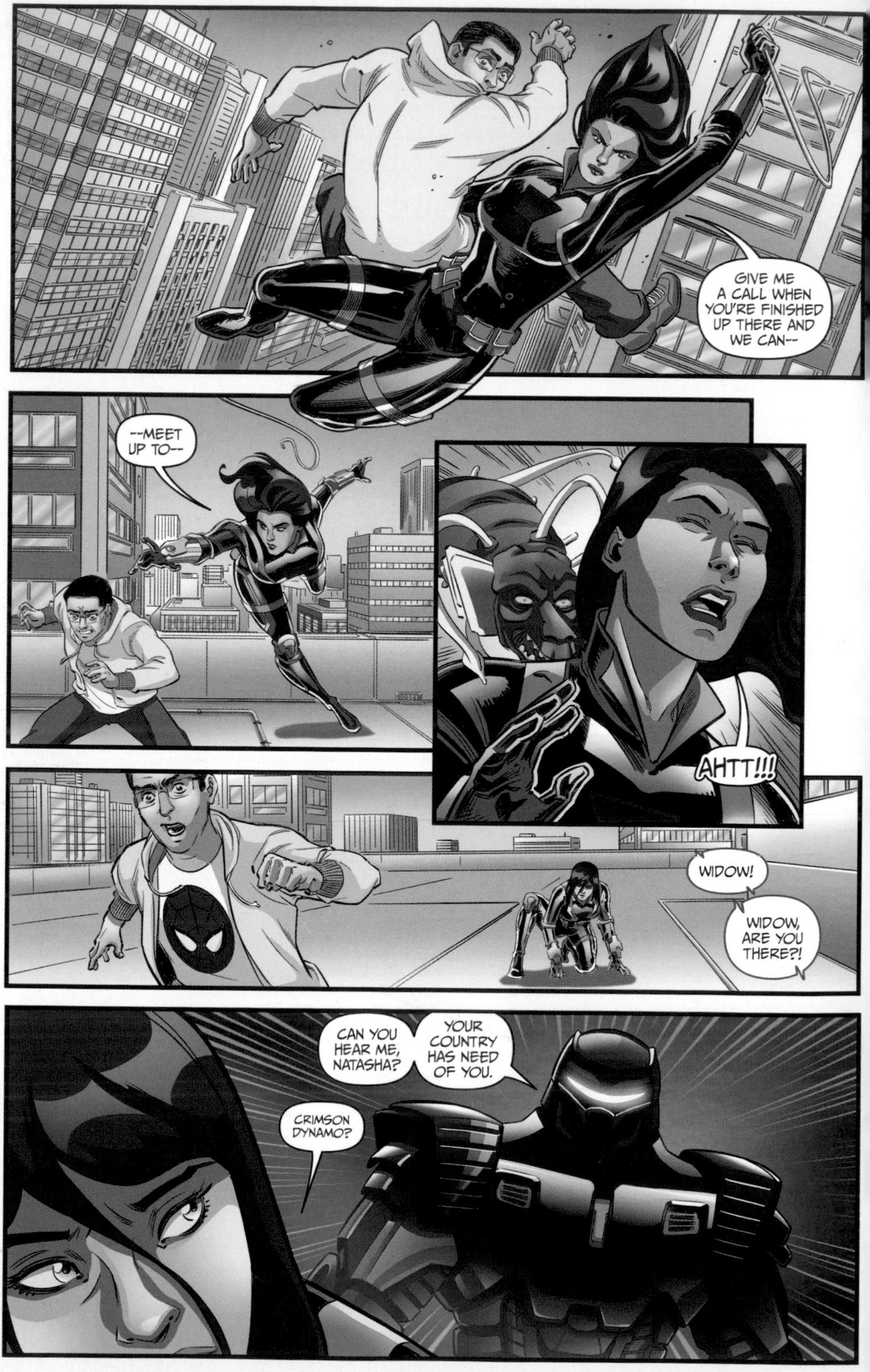
GIVE ME A CALL WHEN YOU'RE FINISHED UP THERE AND WE CAN--
--MEET UP TO--
AHTT!!!
WIDOW!
WIDOW, ARE YOU THERE?!
CAN YOU HEAR ME, NATASHA?
YOUR COUNTRY HAS NEED OF YOU.
CRIMSON DYNAMO?

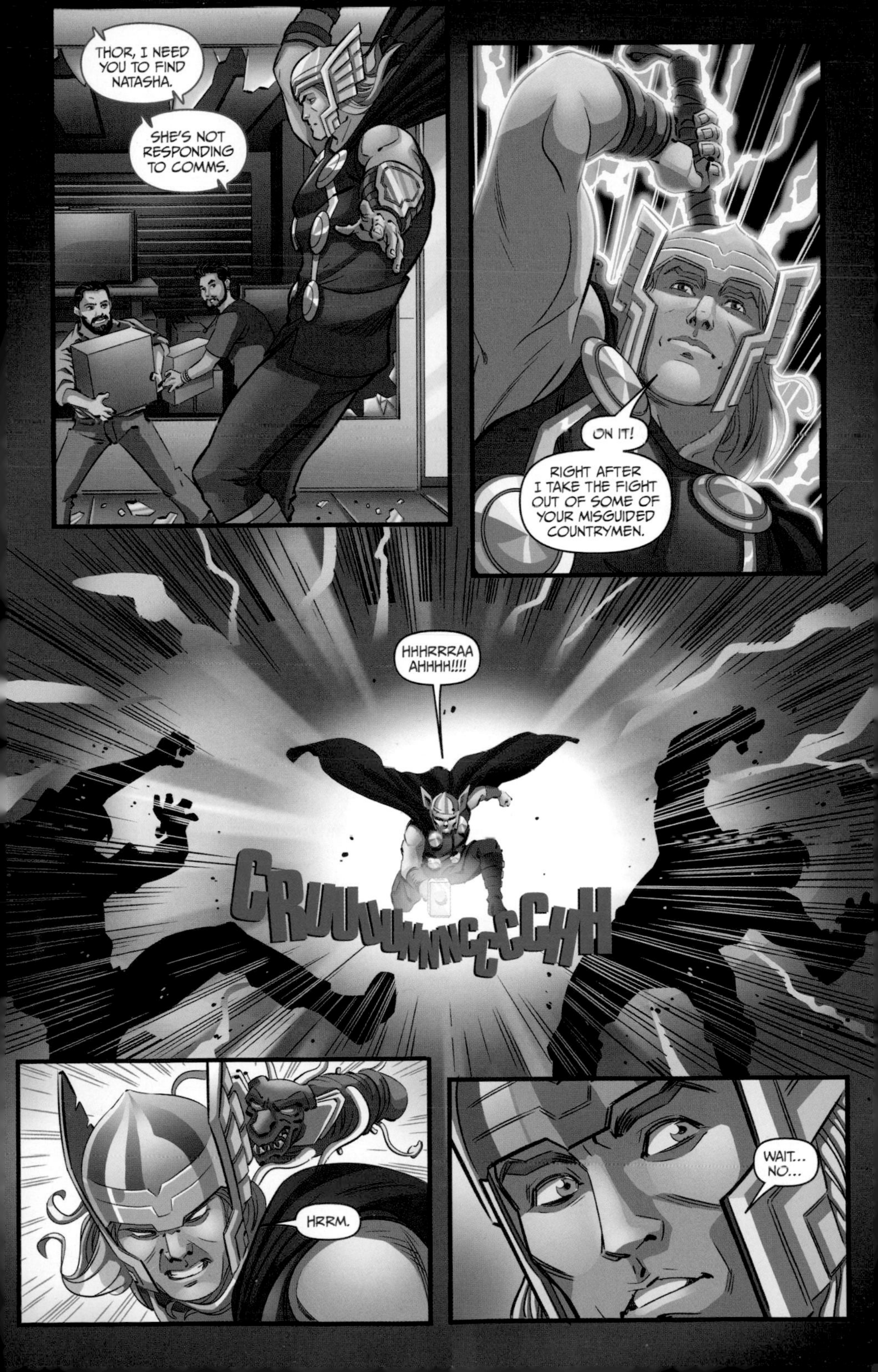
THOR, I NEED YOU TO FIND NATASHA.
SHE'S NOT RESPONDING TO COMMS.
ON IT!
RIGHT AFTER I TAKE THE FIGHT OUT OF SOME OF YOUR MISGUIDED COUNTRYMEN.
HHHRRRAA AHHHH!!!!
CRUUUUNNCCCCHH
HRRM.
WAIT... NO...

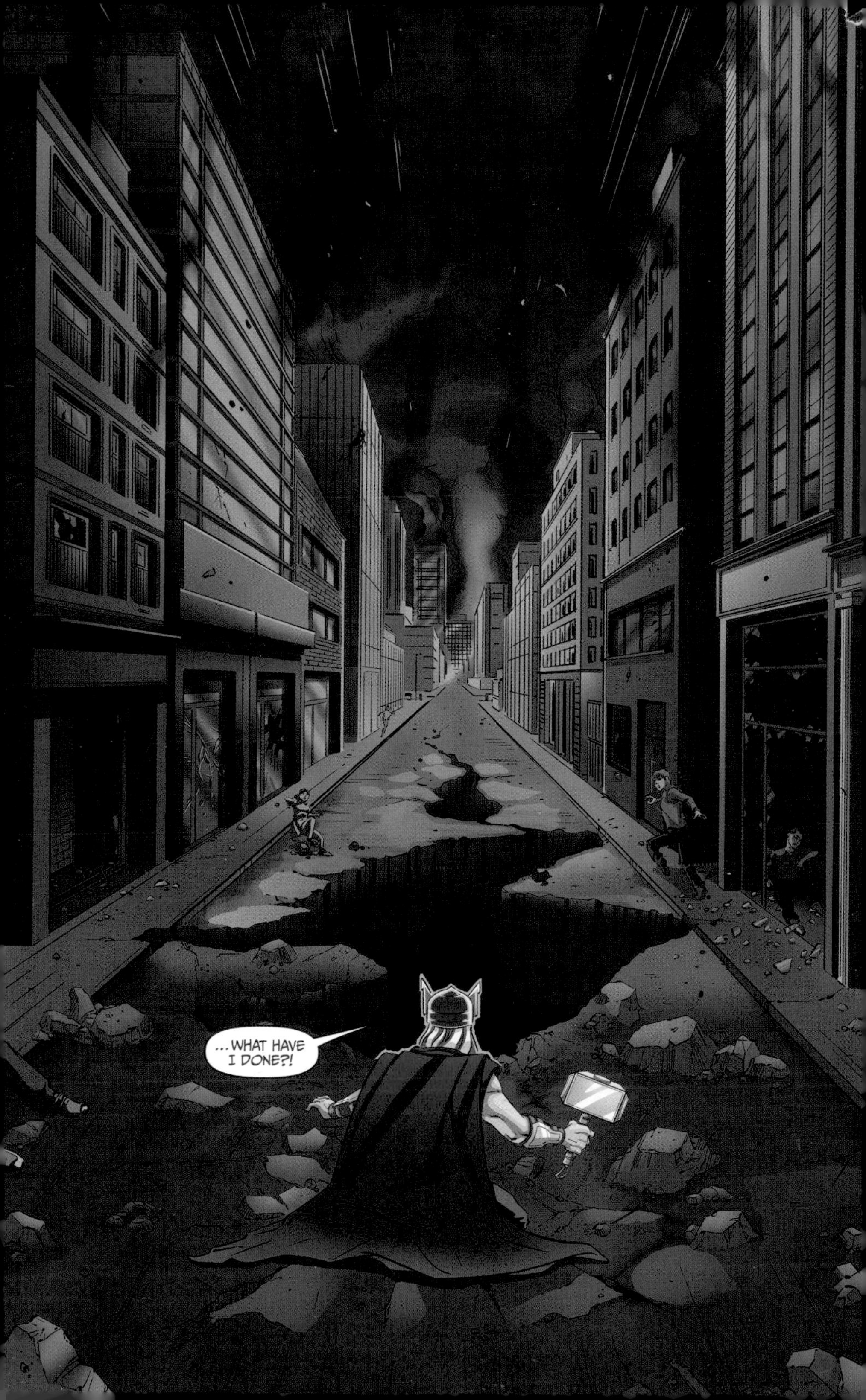
...WHAT HAVE I DONE?!

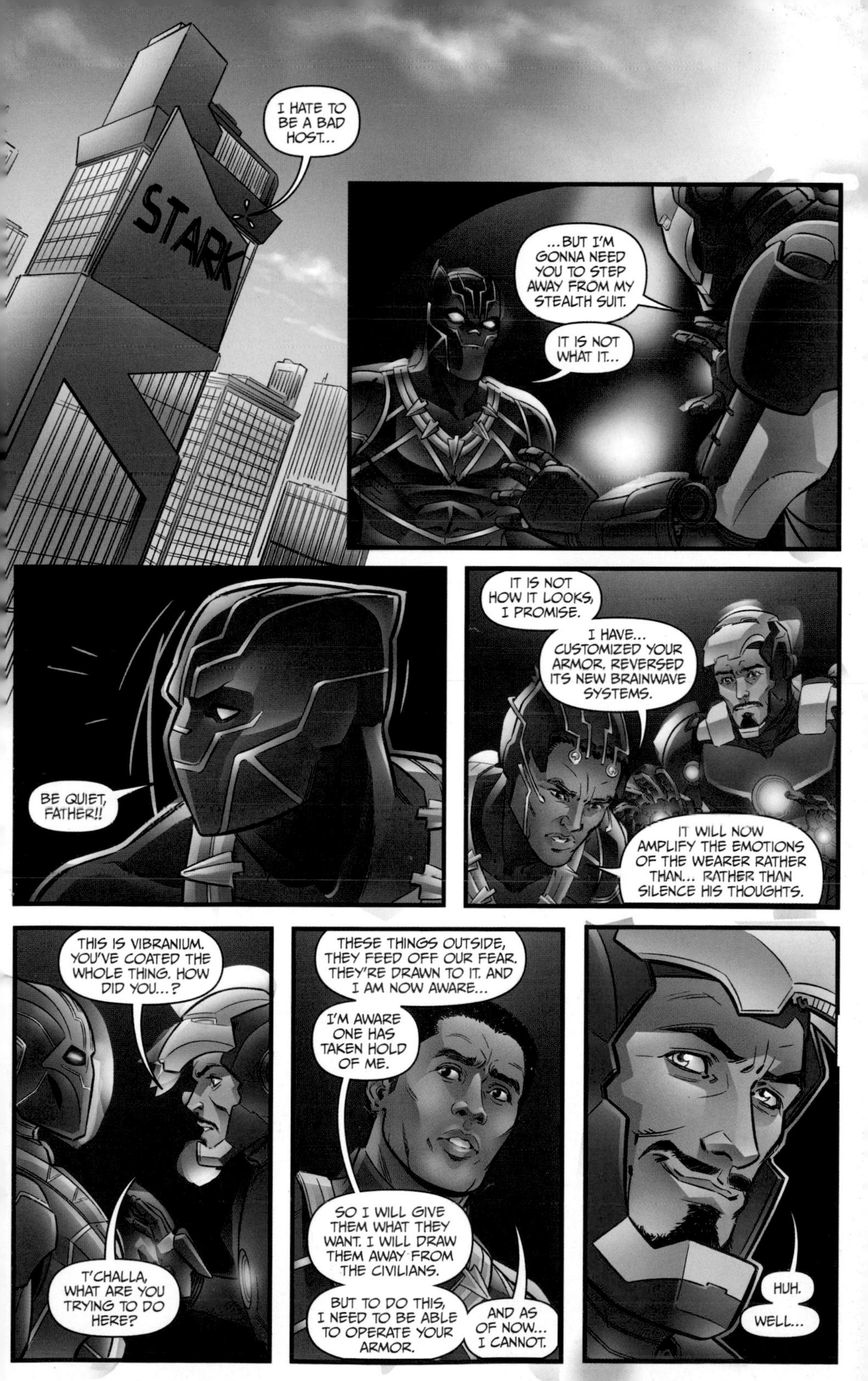
STARK
I HATE TO BE A BAD HOST...
...BUT I'M GONNA NEED YOU TO STEP AWAY FROM MY STEALTH SUIT.
IT IS NOT WHAT IT...
BE QUIET, FATHER!!
IT IS NOT HOW IT LOOKS, I PROMISE.
I HAVE... CUSTOMIZED YOUR ARMOR. REVERSED ITS NEW BRAINWAVE SYSTEMS.
IT WILL NOW AMPLIFY THE EMOTIONS OF THE WEARER RATHER THAN... RATHER THAN SILENCE HIS THOUGHTS.
THIS IS VIBRANIUM. YOU'VE COATED THE WHOLE THING. HOW DID YOU...?
T'CHALLA, WHAT ARE YOU TRYING TO DO HERE?
THESE THINGS OUTSIDE, THEY FEED OFF OUR FEAR. THEY'RE DRAWN TO IT. AND I AM NOW AWARE...
I'M AWARE ONE HAS TAKEN HOLD OF ME.
SO I WILL GIVE THEM WHAT THEY WANT. I WILL DRAW THEM AWAY FROM THE CIVILIANS.
BUT TO DO THIS, I NEED TO BE ABLE TO OPERATE YOUR ARMOR.
AND AS OF NOW... I CANNOT.
HUH.
WELL...

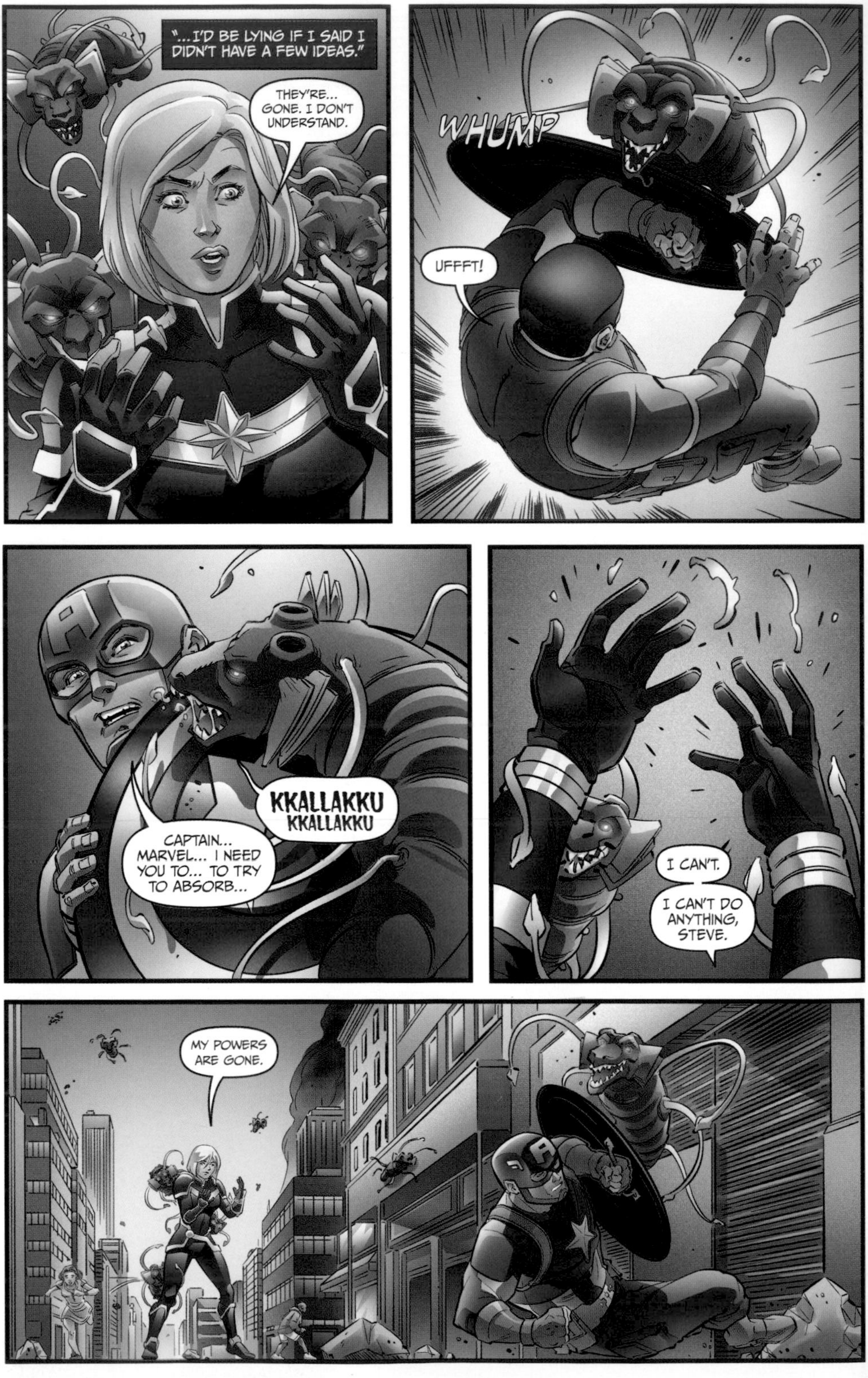
"...I'D BE LYING IF I SAID I DIDN'T HAVE A FEW IDEAS."
THEY'RE... GONE. I DON'T UNDERSTAND.
WHUMP
UFFFT!
KKALLAKKU KKALLAKKU
CAPTAIN... MARVEL... I NEED YOU TO... TO TRY TO ABSORB...
I CAN'T.
I CAN'T DO ANYTHING, STEVE.
MY POWERS ARE GONE.

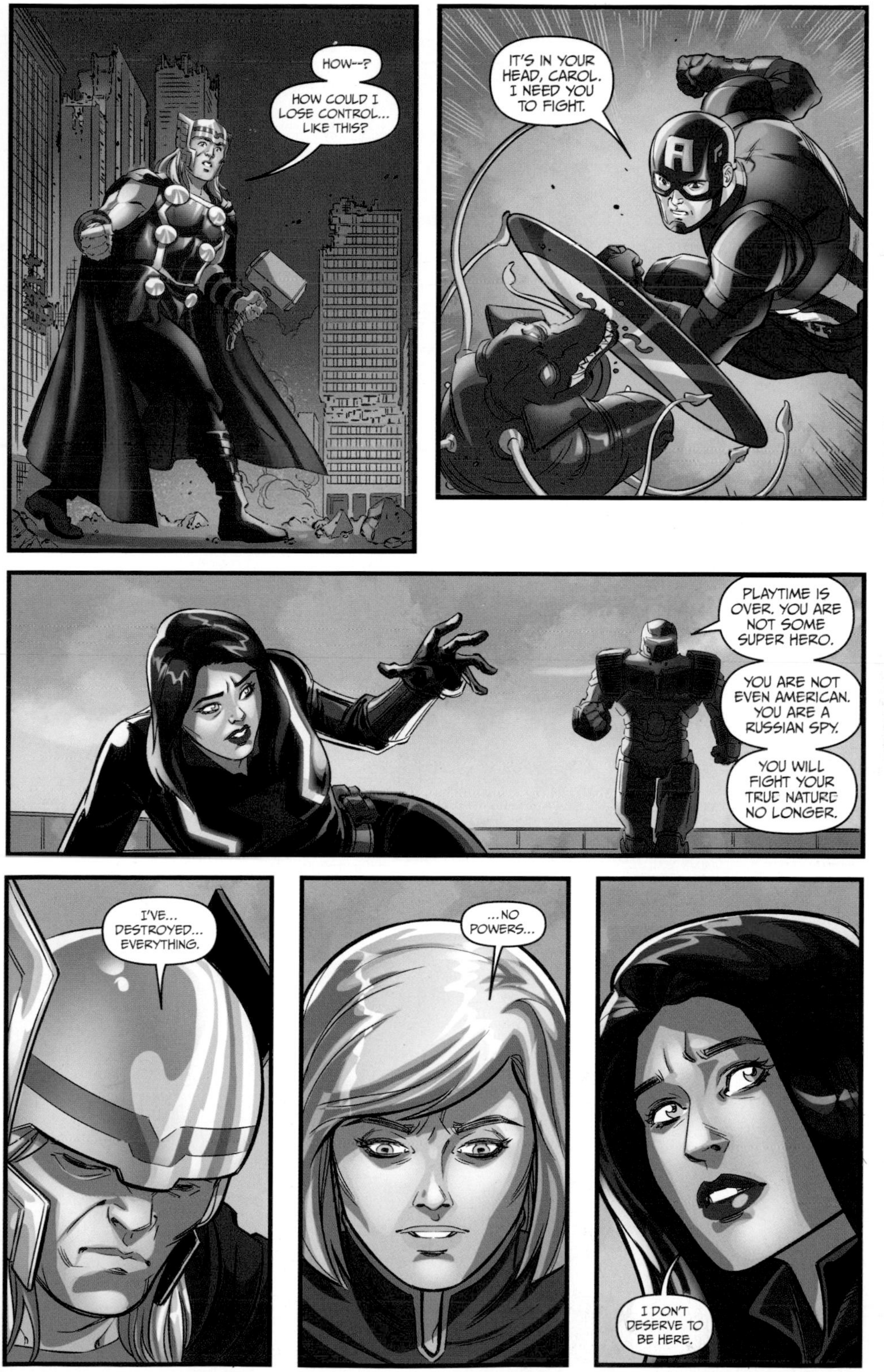
HOW--?
HOW COULD I LOSE CONTROL... LIKE THIS?
IT'S IN YOUR HEAD, CAROL. I NEED YOU TO FIGHT.
PLAYTIME IS OVER. YOU ARE NOT SOME SUPER HERO.
YOU ARE NOT EVEN AMERICAN. YOU ARE A RUSSIAN SPY.
YOU WILL FIGHT YOUR TRUE NATURE NO LONGER.
I'VE... DESTROYED... EVERYTHING.
...NO POWERS...
I DON'T DESERVE TO BE HERE.

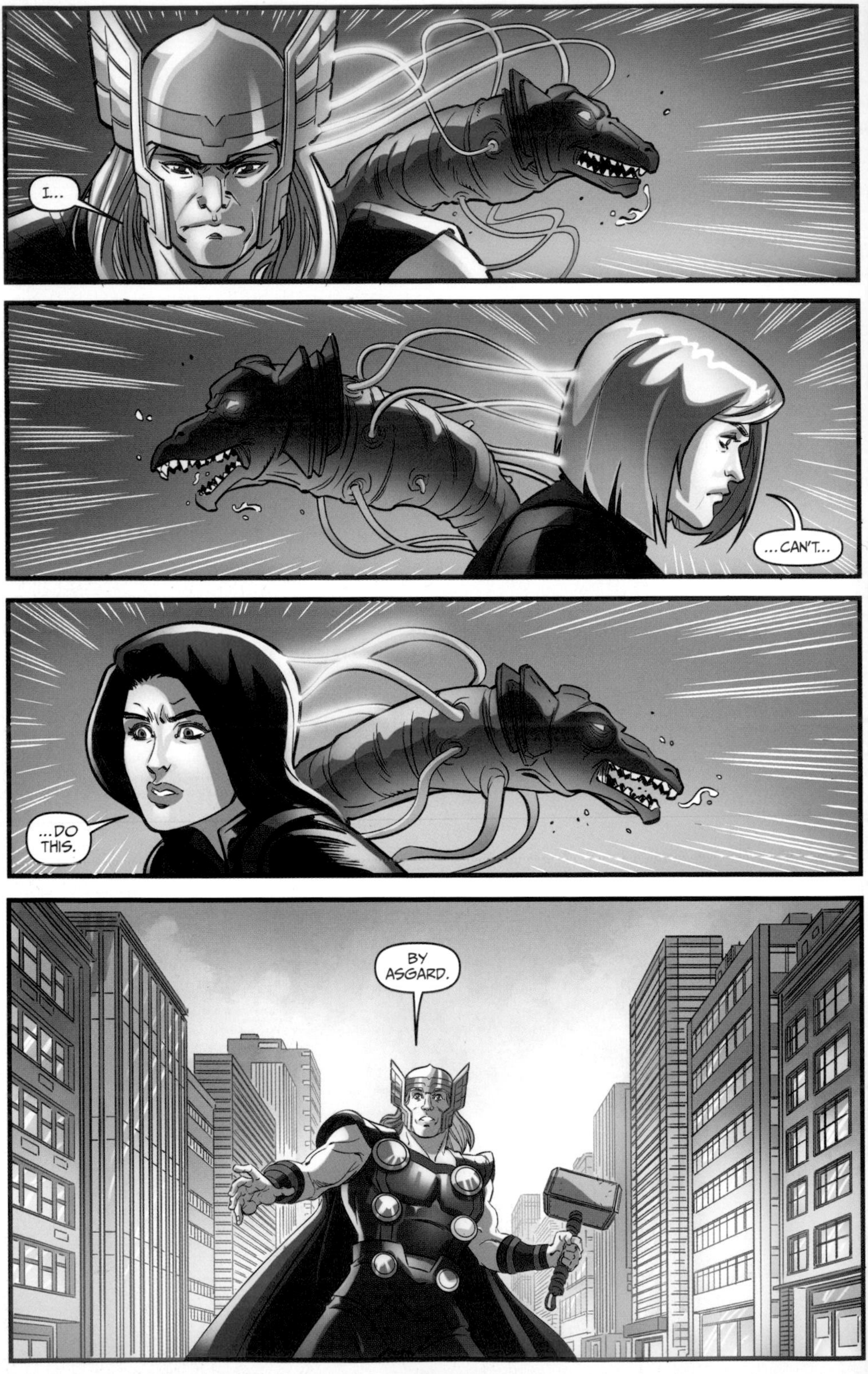
I...
...CAN'T...
...DO THIS.
BY ASGARD.

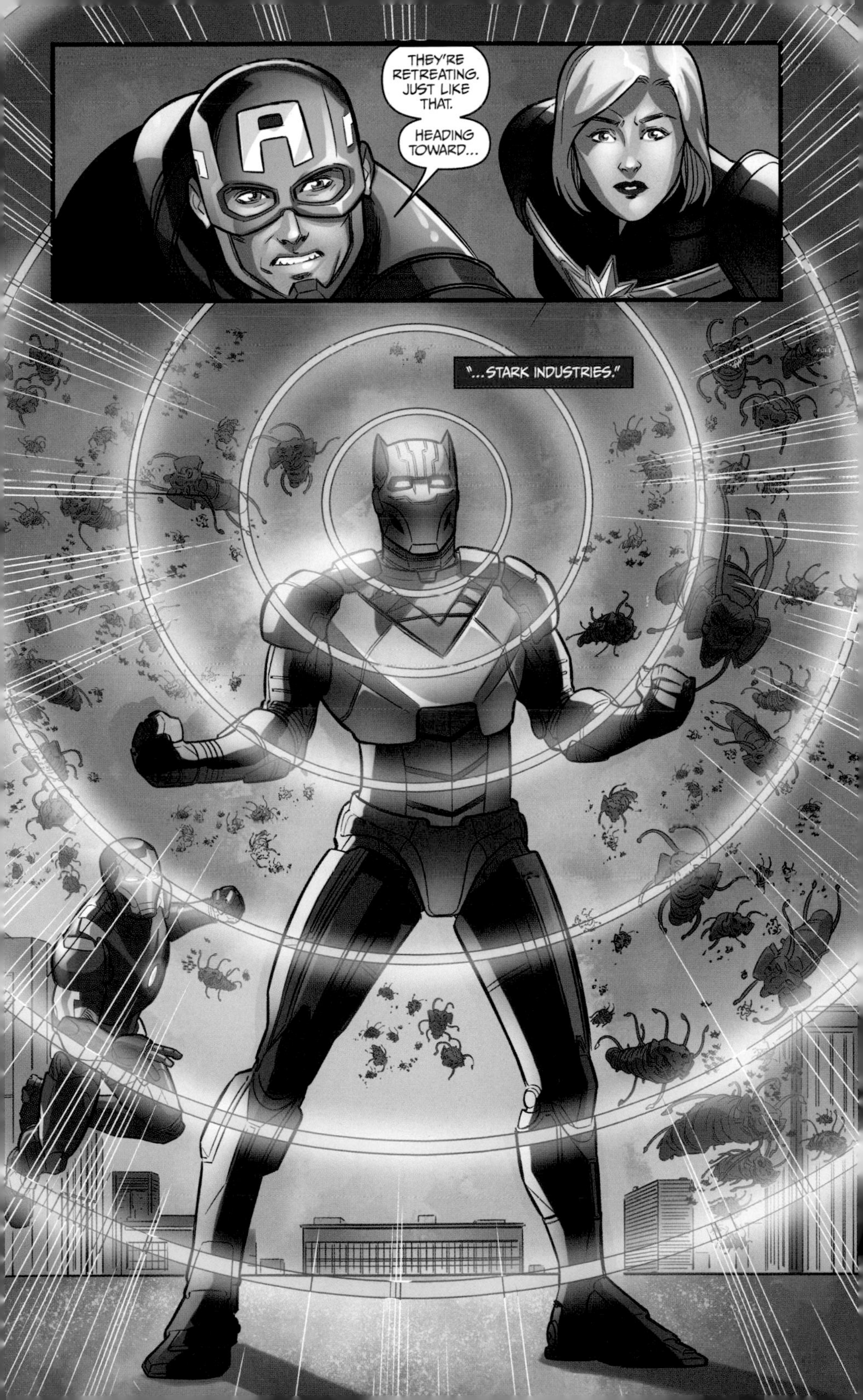
THEY'RE RETREATING. JUST LIKE THAT.
HEADING TOWARD...
"...STARK INDUSTRIES."

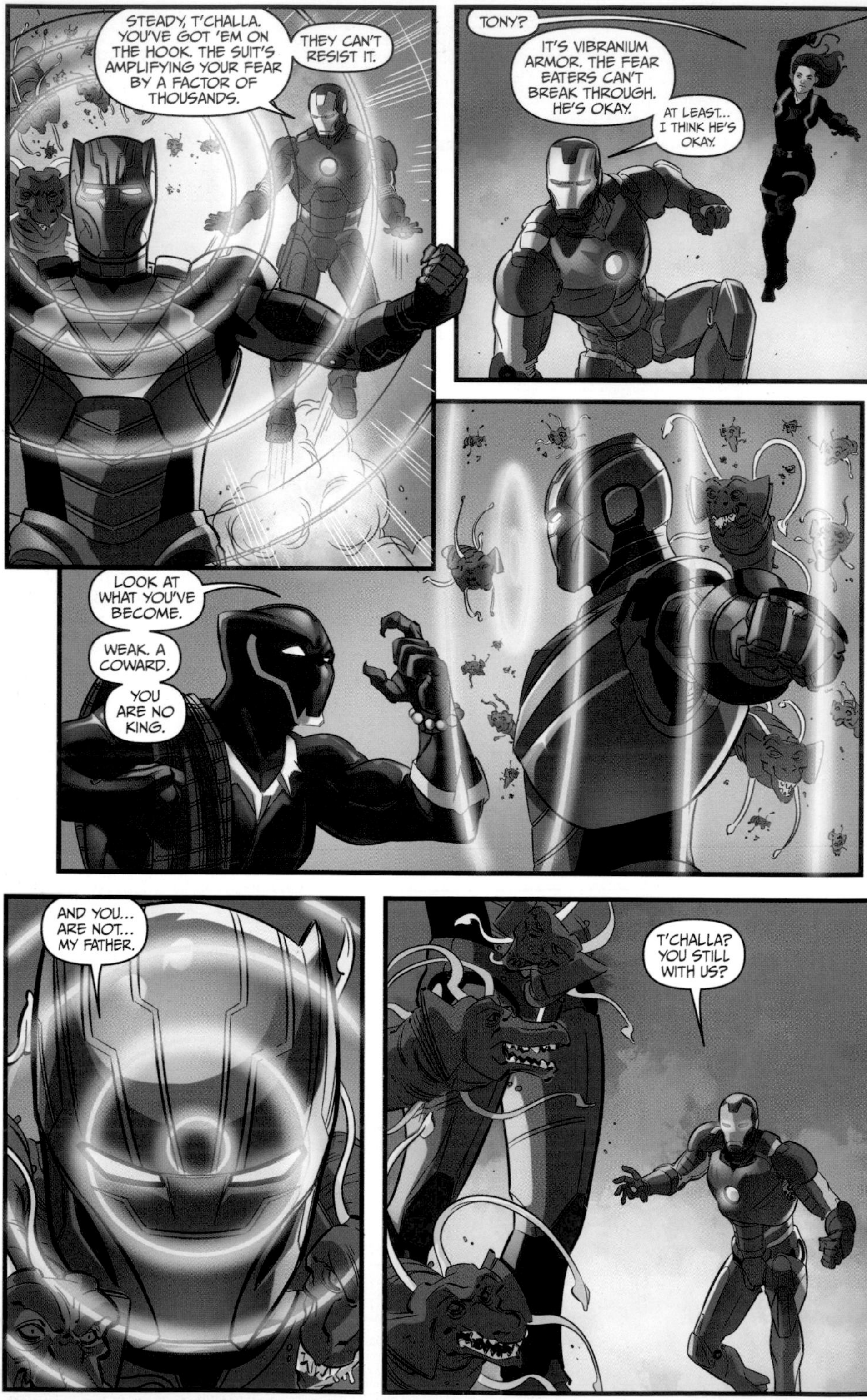
STEADY, T'CHALLA. YOU'VE GOT 'EM ON THE HOOK. THE SUIT'S AMPLIFYING YOUR FEAR BY A FACTOR OF THOUSANDS.
THEY CAN'T RESIST IT.
TONY?
IT'S VIBRANIUM ARMOR. THE FEAR EATERS CAN'T BREAK THROUGH. HE'S OKAY.
AT LEAST... I THINK HE'S OKAY.
LOOK AT WHAT YOU'VE BECOME.
WEAK. A COWARD.
YOU ARE NO KING.
AND YOU... ARE NOT... MY FATHER.
T'CHALLA? YOU STILL WITH US?

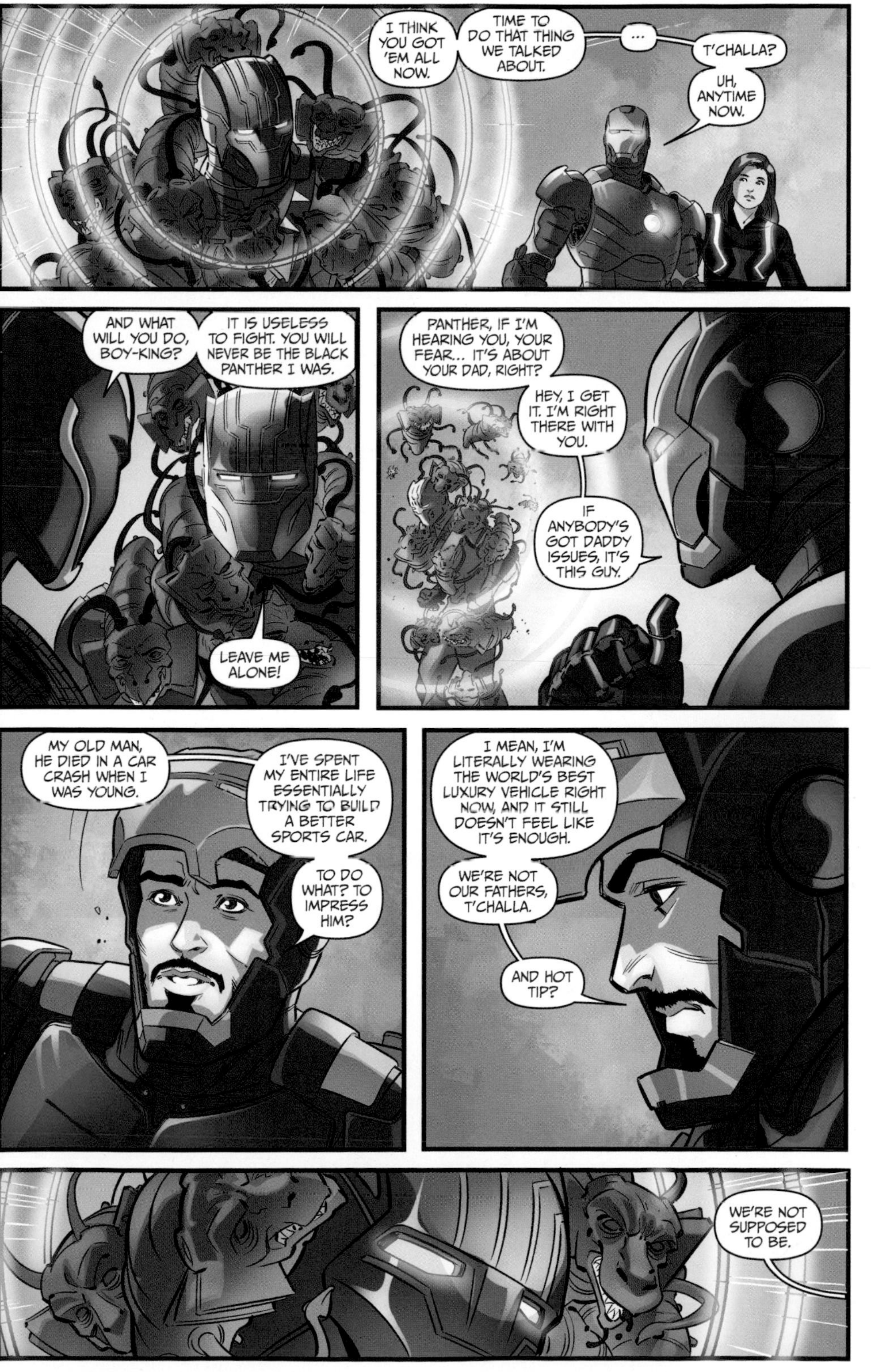
I THINK YOU GOT 'EM ALL NOW.
TIME TO DO THAT THING WE TALKED ABOUT.
...
T'CHALLA?
UH, ANYTIME NOW.
AND WHAT WILL YOU DO, BOY-KING?
IT IS USELESS TO FIGHT. YOU WILL NEVER BE THE BLACK PANTHER I WAS.
LEAVE ME ALONE!
PANTHER, IF I'M HEARING YOU, YOUR FEAR... IT'S ABOUT YOUR DAD, RIGHT?
HEY, I GET IT. I'M RIGHT THERE WITH YOU.
IF ANYBODY'S GOT DADDY ISSUES, IT'S THIS GUY.
MY OLD MAN, HE DIED IN A CAR CRASH WHEN I WAS YOUNG.
I'VE SPENT MY ENTIRE LIFE ESSENTIALLY TRYING TO BUILD A BETTER SPORTS CAR.
TO DO WHAT? TO IMPRESS HIM?
I MEAN, I'M LITERALLY WEARING THE WORLD'S BEST LUXURY VEHICLE RIGHT NOW, AND IT STILL DOESN'T FEEL LIKE IT'S ENOUGH.
WE'RE NOT OUR FATHERS, T'CHALLA.
AND HOT TIP?
WE'RE NOT SUPPOSED TO BE.

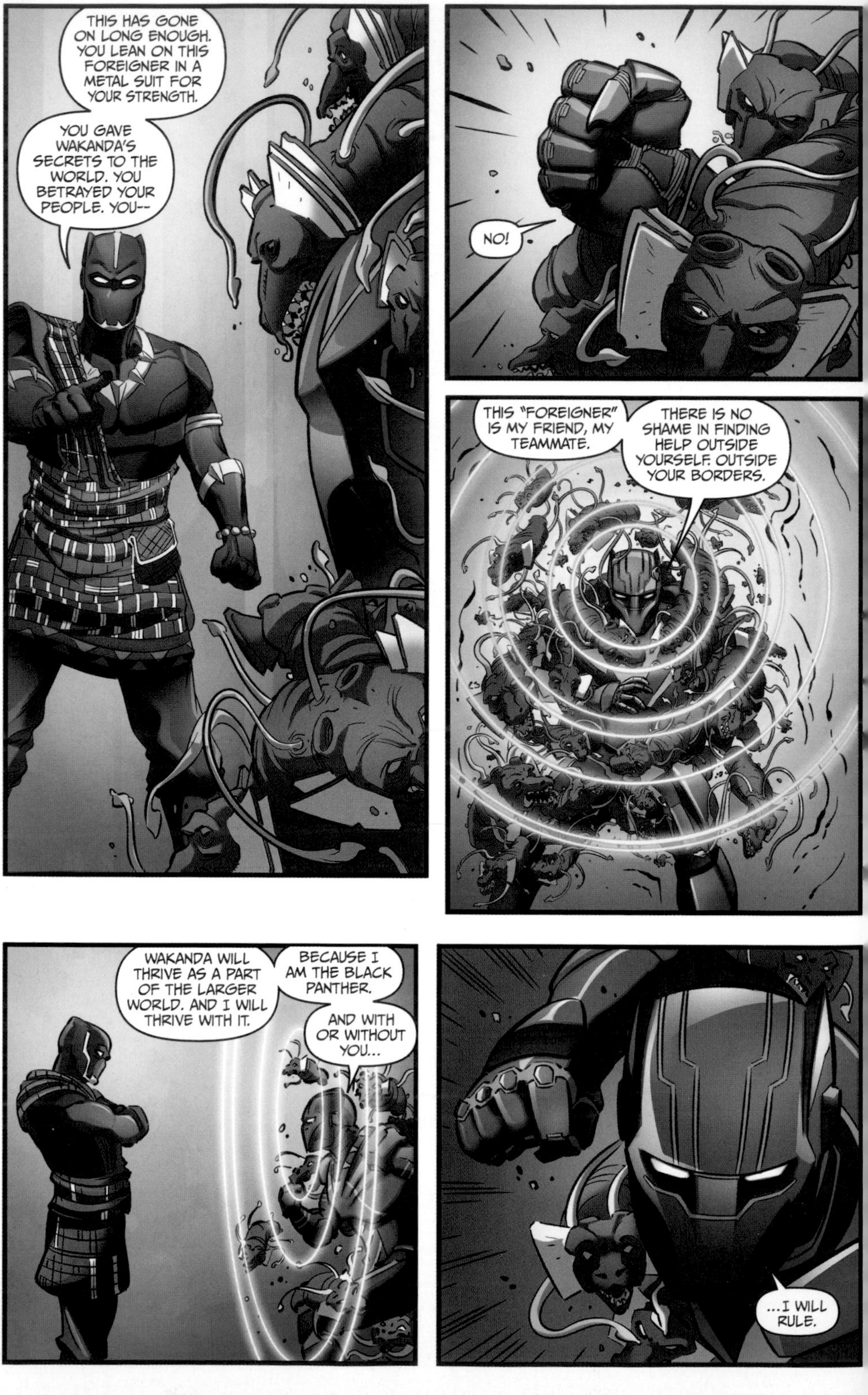
THIS HAS GONE ON LONG ENOUGH. YOU LEAN ON THIS FOREIGNER IN A METAL SUIT FOR YOUR STRENGTH.
YOU GAVE WAKANDA'S SECRETS TO THE WORLD. YOU BETRAYED YOUR PEOPLE. YOU--
NO!
THIS "FOREIGNER" IS MY FRIEND, MY TEAMMATE.
THERE IS NO SHAME IN FINDING HELP OUTSIDE YOURSELF. OUTSIDE YOUR BORDERS.
WAKANDA WILL THRIVE AS A PART OF THE LARGER WORLD. AND I WILL THRIVE WITH IT.
BECAUSE I AM THE BLACK PANTHER.
AND WITH OR WITHOUT YOU...
...I WILL RULE.

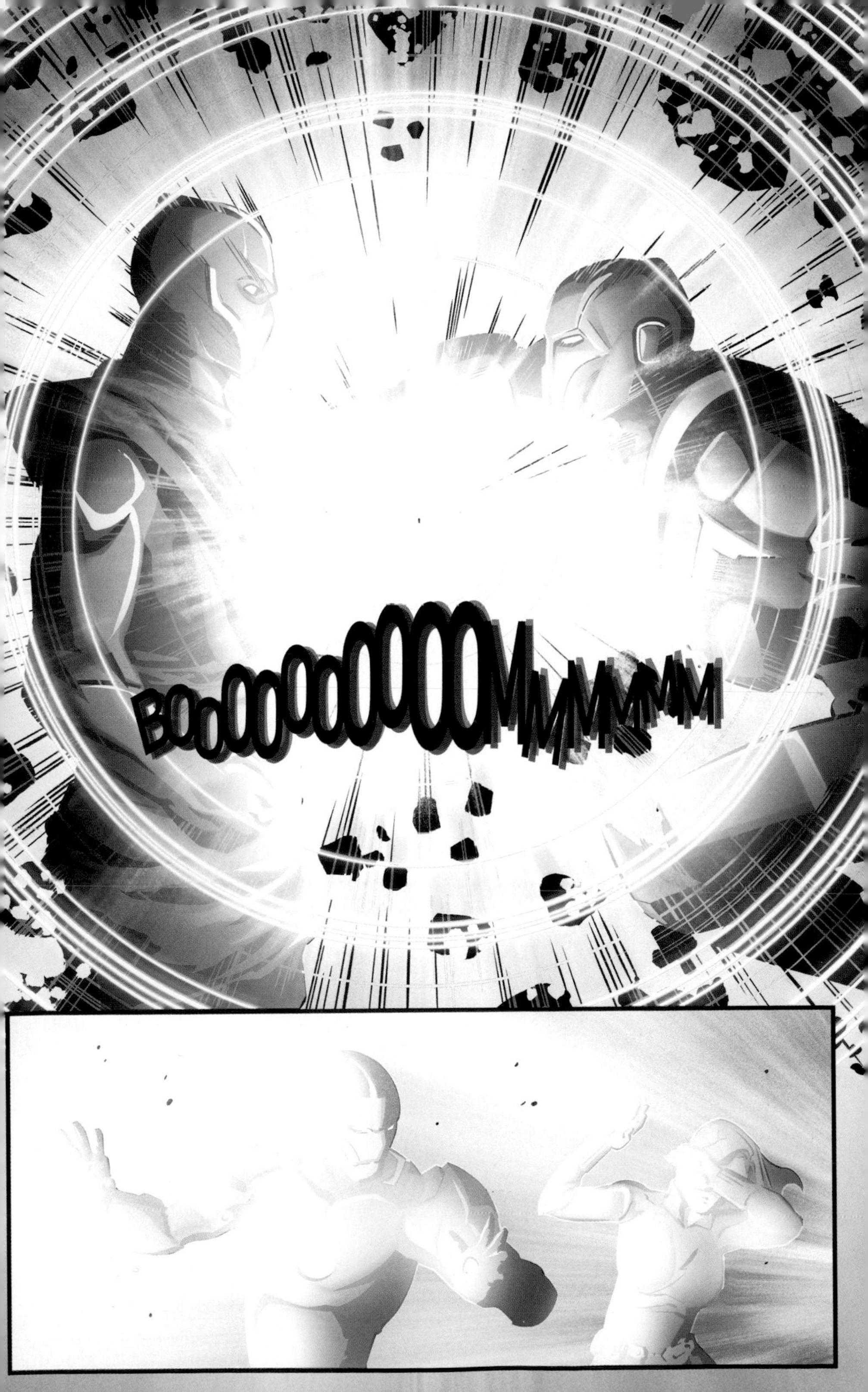
BOOOOOOOOOOMMMMMMM

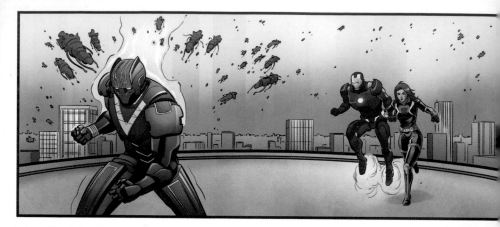

I GOT YOU.

NICE WORK.

AGH!

GET IT ALL OUT OF YOUR SYSTEM.

BUT ALSO, WARN ME NEXT TIME.

BECAUSE, GROSS.

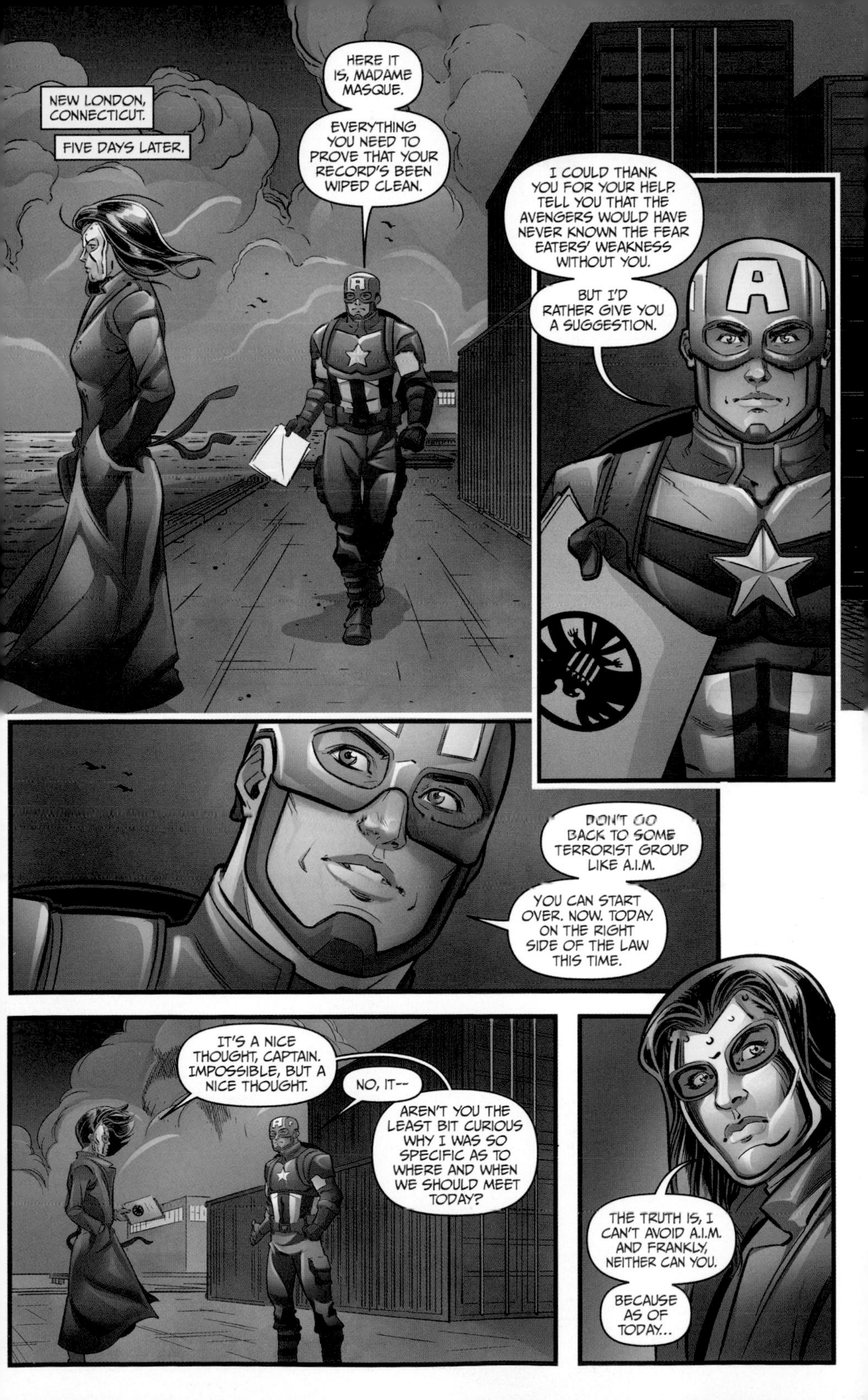
NEW LONDON, CONNECTICUT.
FIVE DAYS LATER.
HERE IT IS, MADAME MASQUE.
EVERYTHING YOU NEED TO PROVE THAT YOUR RECORD'S BEEN WIPED CLEAN.
I COULD THANK YOU FOR YOUR HELP. TELL YOU THAT THE AVENGERS WOULD HAVE NEVER KNOWN THE FEAR EATERS' WEAKNESS WITHOUT YOU.
BUT I'D RATHER GIVE YOU A SUGGESTION.
DON'T GO BACK TO SOME TERRORIST GROUP LIKE A.I.M.
YOU CAN START OVER. NOW. TODAY. ON THE RIGHT SIDE OF THE LAW THIS TIME.
IT'S A NICE THOUGHT, CAPTAIN. IMPOSSIBLE, BUT A NICE THOUGHT.
NO, IT--
AREN'T YOU THE LEAST BIT CURIOUS WHY I WAS SO SPECIFIC AS TO WHERE AND WHEN WE SHOULD MEET TODAY?
THE TRUTH IS, I CAN'T AVOID A.I.M. AND FRANKLY, NEITHER CAN YOU.
BECAUSE AS OF TODAY...

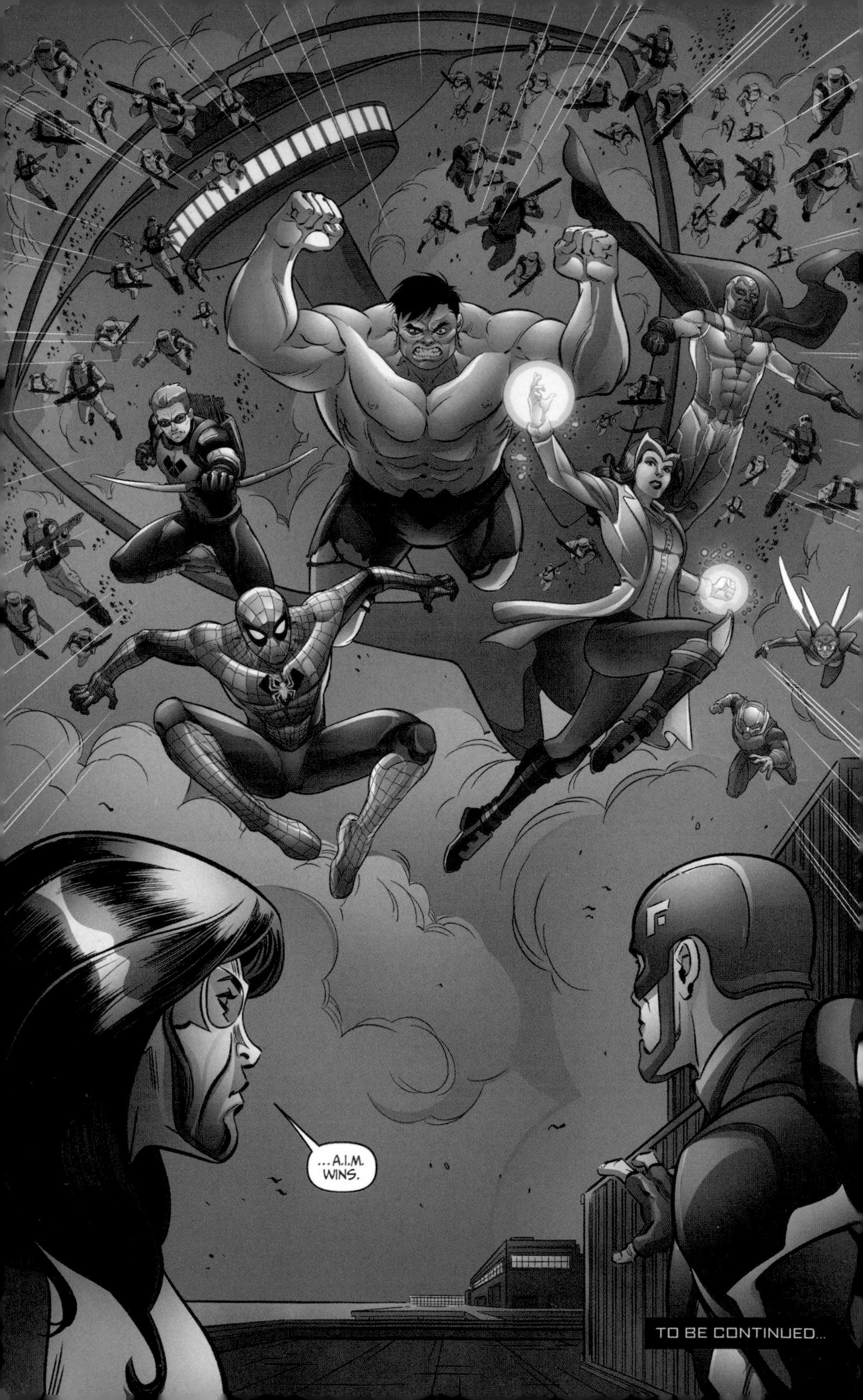
...A.I.M.
WINS.
TO BE CONTINUED...

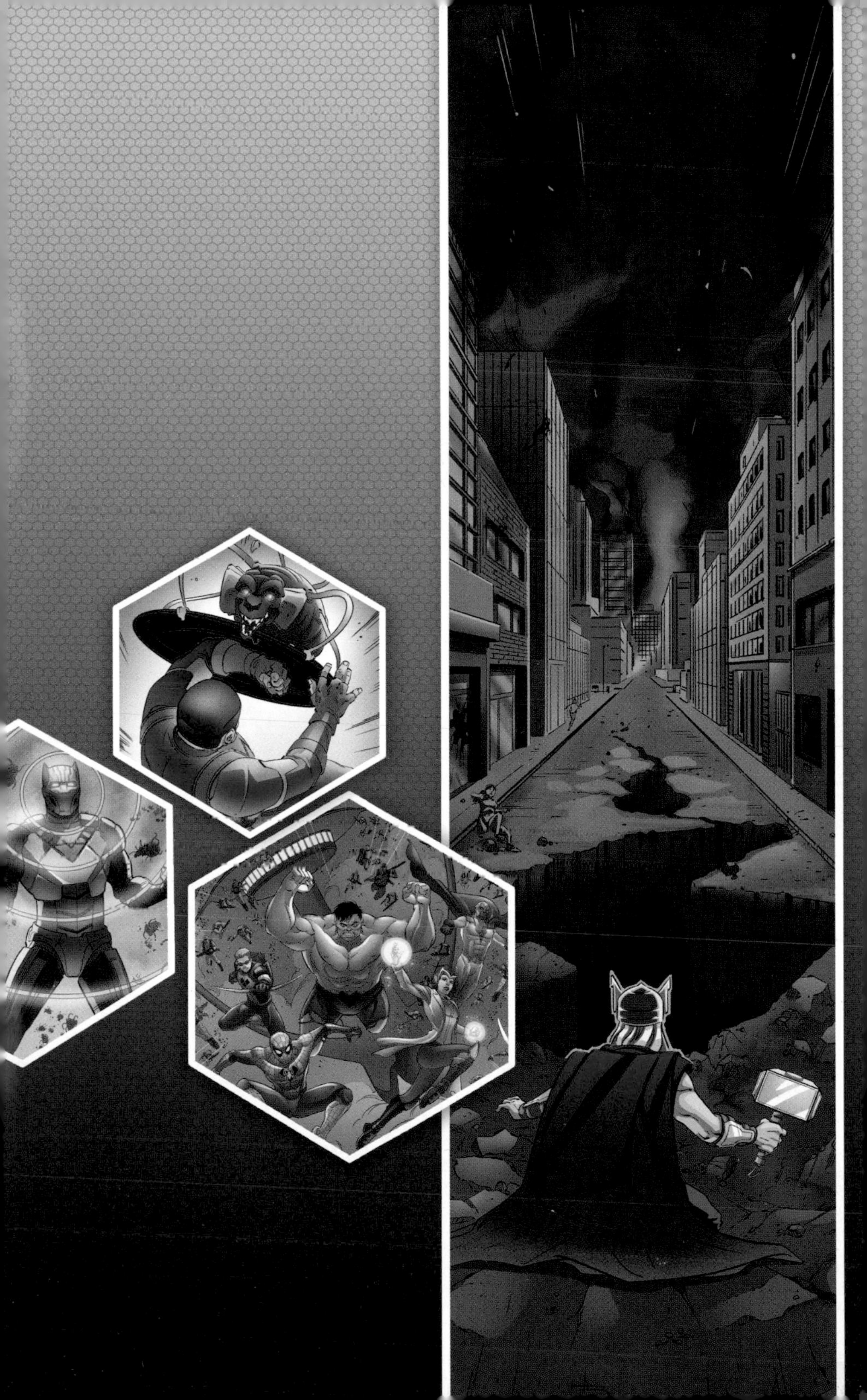

ART BY: BEN HARVEY

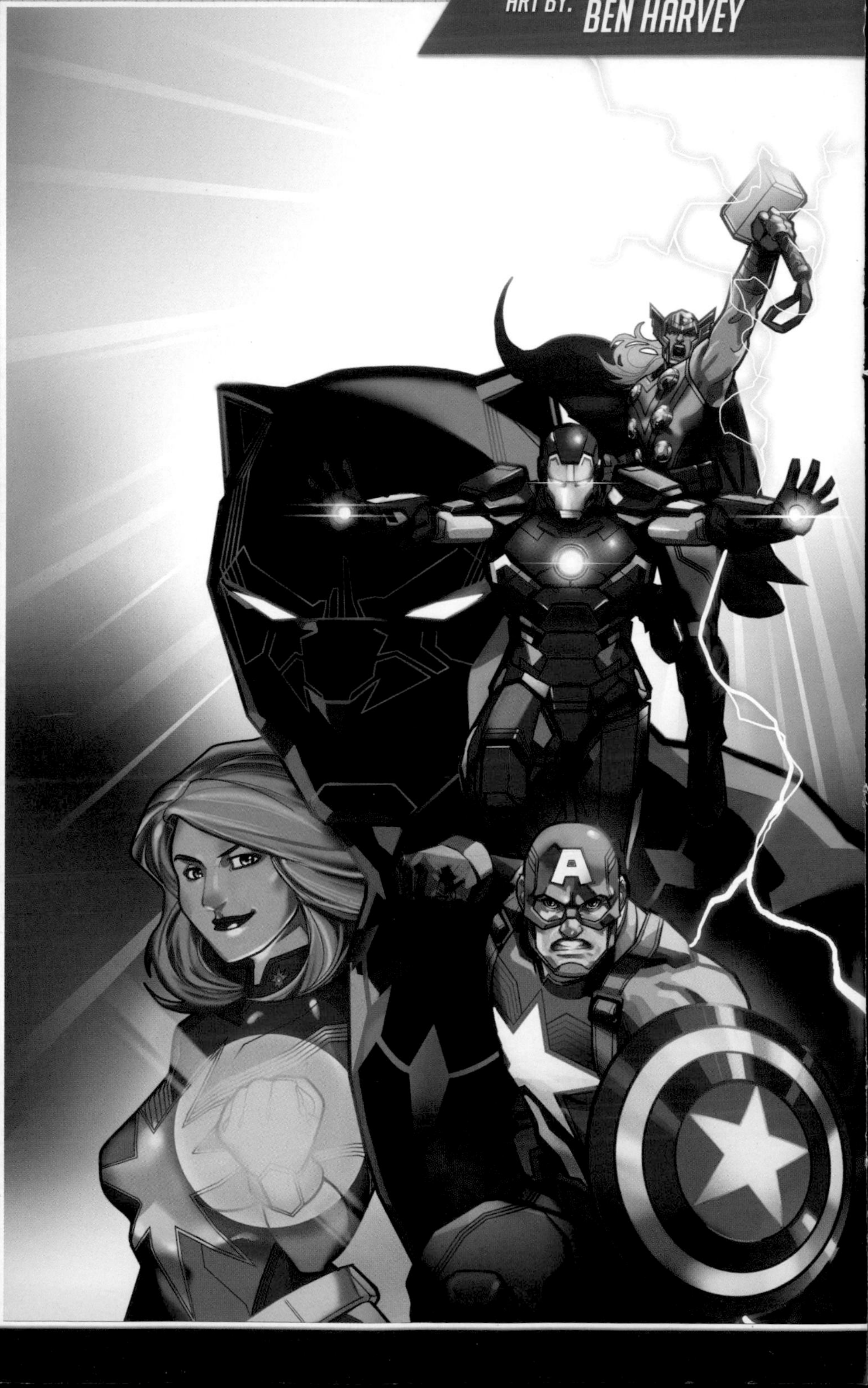

ART BY: DARIO BRIZUELA

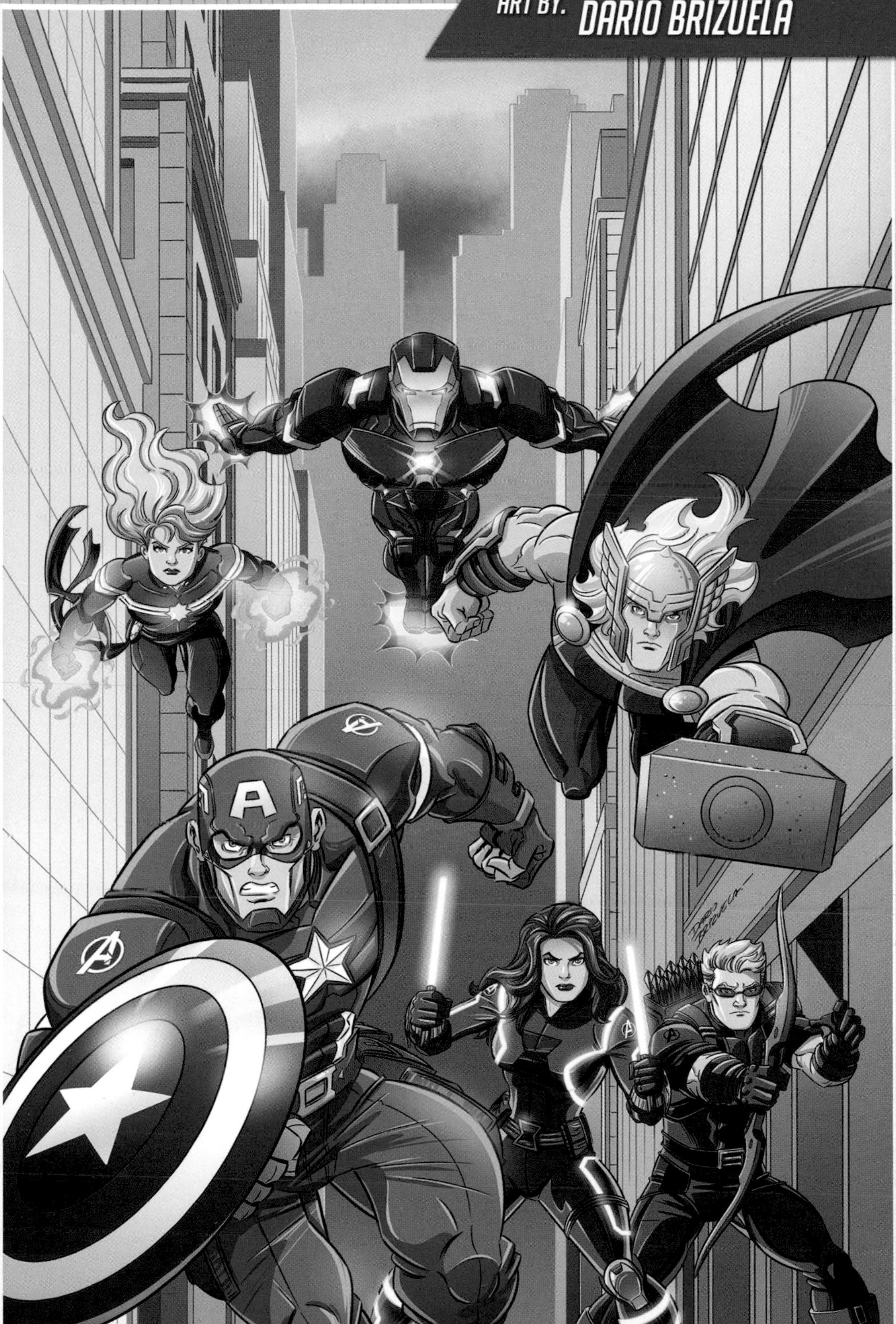

ART BY: SIOBHAN KEENAN

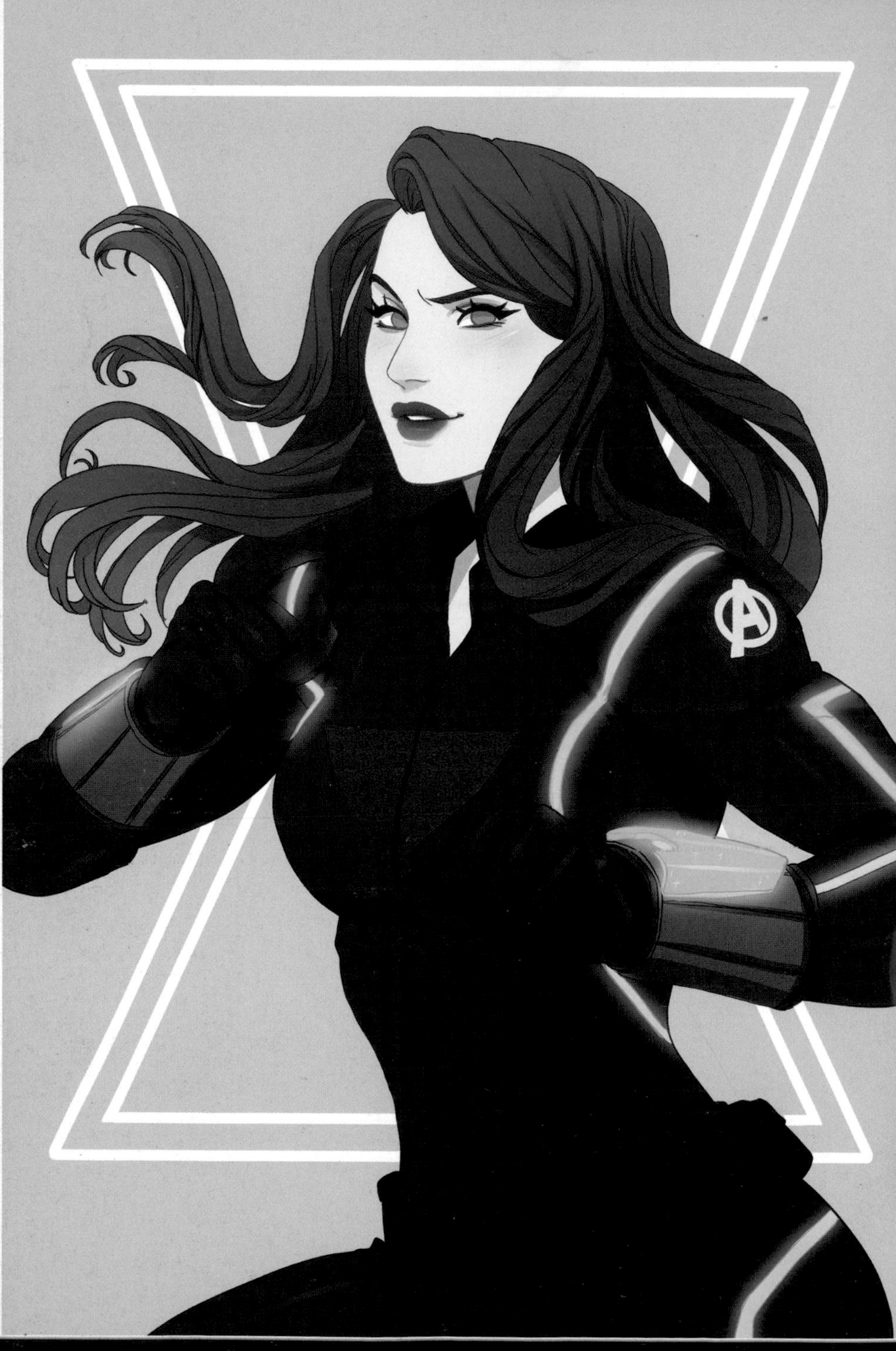